Praise for
Signed, Skye Harper

"Winston's confusion over growing up, falling in love,
and discovering her family is seamlessly woven into an
emotional coming-of-age story. With a balance of family
drama and humor, Winston's journey never feels forced. . . .
A lovely addition to a collection of family stories."
—*Booklist*

"[Winston's] voice is distinctive, cadenced, and packed
with emotion. . . . On this first-love, coming-of-age road
trip, it's a pleasure to be along for the ride."
—*Horn Book*

Signed,
Skye Harper

Also by CAROL LYNCH WILLIAMS

Glimpse
Waiting

Signed, Skye Harper

Carol Lynch Williams

A Paula Wiseman Book

SIMON & SCHUSTER BFYR

NEW YORK • LONDON • TORONTO • SYDNEY • NEW DELHI

An imprint of Simon & Schuster Children's Publishing Division

1230 Avenue of the Americas, New York, New York 10020

SIMON & SCHUSTER BFYR is a trademark of Simon & Schuster, Inc.

For information about special discounts for bulk purchases, please contact Simon & Schuster Special Sales at 1-866-506-1949 or business@simonandschuster.com.

The Simon & Schuster Speakers Bureau can bring authors to your live event. For more information or to book an event, contact the Simon & Schuster Speakers Bureau at 1-866-248-3049 or visit our website at www.simonspeakers.com.

Also available in a SIMON & SCHUSTER BFYR hardcover edition

Cover design by Krista Vossen

Interior design by Hilary Zarycky

The text for this book is set in Bembo.

Manufactured in the United States of America

First SIMON & SCHUSTER BFYR paperback edition May 2015

2 4 6 8 10 9 7 5 3 1

The Library of Congress has cataloged the hardcover edition as follows:

Williams, Carol Lynch.

Signed, Skye Harper / Carol Lynch Williams. — First edition.

pages cm

"A Paula Wiseman Book."

Summary: In 1972, while her idol, Mark Spitz, is in Germany competing in the Olympics, fifteen-year-old Winston, her Nanny, and her crush, Steve, head to Las Vegas in Steve's parents' motor home to reconnect with Winston's mother, who left ten years before to become a star.

ISBN 978-1-4814-0032-9 (hardback) — ISBN 978-1-4814-0034-3 (eBook)

[1. Mothers and daughters—Fiction. 2. Grandmothers—Fiction.

3. Dating (Social customs)—Fiction.

4. Automobile travel—Fiction. 5. Swimming—Fiction.] I. Title.

PZ7.W65588Sig 2014

[Fic]—dc23

2013040091

ISBN 978-1-4814-0033-6 (pbk)

For Stephen Fraser

Signed,
Skye Harper

1

Surprise

Nanny sat at the kitchen table when I wandered in at dusk from swimming, not a light in the house on, just a cigarette glowing.

"Hey, Winston girl," she said. "You got a minute?"

She didn't sound too happy. In fact, I'd say she sounded right miserable. I strained to see more than the glow of her ciggie but was hypnotized by the red burn.

Blinking, I said, "What's wrong?" I slid onto the rattan chair, my behind almost not making it. My chlorine-smelling swimsuit made my shorts and T-shirt wet. I let out a sigh. Since turning fifteen, I've found myself sighing an awful lot. That's my family's fault.

I helped myself to one of the biscuits from breakfast, the pan covered with a cloth so they wouldn't dry out hard as rocks. It was like biting into a brick. The cloth hadn't helped at all. I sighed again. Then let out an "I'm starving."

"Stop that damn sighing," Nanny said. "You're breathing up way more than your fair share of oxygen." She drew long on her cigarette. Her face lit up in such a way she looked like a demon, shadowed eyes and all. But who's allowed to tell their grandmother that kind of thing? "Dinner's on the stove, but wait it out a minute. I got to tell you something."

"Tell then," I said. "School starts in a couple of weeks and I got things to do before then."

"Smart butt," Nanny said, and ground out her cigarette.

I smiled. So she wasn't too bad off. Nanny only uses the word "butt" if she's talking about her Winstons-taste-good-like . . . You know what I'm saying. And yes, I was named after the cigarette, but I've told no one that fact, not even my very best friend, Patty Bailey, who is tall as an oak tree and gone to Louisiana for the summer. "Butt" is about her only swear. Nanny's. Not Patty's. That's an almost truth.

"Nanny," I said, "what's got your goat? Sure I can't fill a plate while I listen to you jaw?"

"Yes, I'm sure." Nanny slapped at the table, and Denny, our rooster, ruffled his feathers and clucked in his throat. I hadn't even known he was there. I settled in my chair and waited—keeping the sigh tucked in tight—and pulled at my T-shirt to loosen it some.

Nanny took in a breath.

"I got a letter from your momma."

Hmmmm.

So that's why she was sitting in the dark. Nanny, not Momma.

"Tell me more." I said those words, though I didn't mean them.

Cold-water feeling covered me from my ankles up. It

was like the time I got baptized. That day, the water heater was broke, and no one knew till the preacher and me stepped into the font. Not a thing like the lakes around here, which can be warm as bath water. "Where is she this time?"

Momma's been gone since I turned four. She travels all over the West Coast, sending us postcards. But she never mails a letter unless there's an emergency. Sounded like something big had happened.

I swallowed.

"She need money?"

I heard Nanny working at her pack of cigarettes. Heard her strike the match (saw her face go beastly in the sputter of light), then she started smoking again.

"That's a bad habit," I said. "You want me to take that up? And at almost fifty cents a pack?"

"Stunts your growth," Nanny said. "And I'll beat you with a stick if you start smoking. You know I'm trying to quit."

This is true. Nanny is down from two packs a day to 1.3.

"Let me hear what she says," I said. Then I closed my eyes tight, 'cause this couldn't be anything good.

2
The Letter

Aug 25, 1972

Dear Family (that means you momma and little Winston)—

I done run aground here in Vegas.

The traveling is good but has started to sour. Seems there is no more money to be made out here in the wild, wild west. I've done dancing and singing and even a bit part or two. But what I need is my girls.

Yes, you 2.

The money jar, though, has run dry and there aint a red cent in it.

What do you 2 say about comming to git me?

We could be home by Winston's birthday.

Hows the Blue Goose? Still running good? I had to sell the Lemon. I better go.

Signed,

Skye Harper (who used to be known as Judith Lee Fletcher)

PS Come git me.

3

The Letter, Part Two

If Nanny knew I was reading the letter again, the fourteenth time, this time in bed with a flashlight, she would have shouted, *Do you know how much batteries cost?*

I *don't* know, though you'd think so the way my grandmother is always quoting me prices. "Don't you waste that cereal milk. It's running almost a dollar a gallon." "Eat the crust of that jelly sandwich, girl. That loaf a bread cost me thirty-seven cents." She even knows egg prices, and we got thirteen chickens (sixty-two cents for a dozen large, white eggs—"Though anyone in her right mind knows brown eggs're better.").

I read the letter once more, then folded it and slid it under my pillow. I snapped off the flashlight, sighing. Again.

Bothered.

Ruffled like Denny.

Outside a late-night storm drew near. If I waited, I could go over Momma's words when lightning struck close by. But I wouldn't. Fourteen readings was enough. And anyway, I'd memorized the line that mattered most. *What do you 2 say about comming to git me?* And the other was stuck in my brain too. *But what I need is my girls.*

So what *did* we say about it?

I folded my arms underneath my head and stared at the ceiling.

Nanny hadn't spoken a word when I'd said, "She wants to come back? Back here? To live? In this house? With us? Here? Momma? I mean Skye Harper?" No, Nanny just sucked on the cigarette and looked off over my shoulder at the TV that wasn't even on. Maybe she wanted to watch *Let's Make a Deal*, though that wouldn't show again until tomorrow.

Now the lightning snapped and thunder crashed. Damp air blew in my room, pushing the curtains out like the skirt of an old-timey dancer.

I rolled on my side.

What do you 2 say about comming to git me? That was the last thing I wondered as I fell asleep.

4

Thelma Dog

Momma wore a curtain for a skirt.

"Couldn't get a job," she said. Cigarette smoke filled the room. It was hot in here. Hot like an electric blanket and itchy like the blanket was wool, too.

I didn't answer.

"I said I'd be back," Momma said. She let out a long whine, like she was nervous or something.

When I opened my mouth, it was big enough for a train to pass through. Words tumbled out, written in half cursive, half print. "Go away," they said.

Thunder over the house, maybe in the front room, rattled me awake.

Right next to me, there in my bed, though it wasn't allowed, was Thelma, our pup who hasn't been a pup in six years.

"Get off me, girl," I said, pushing her body away. She refused to move as the sky lit up and thunder crashed in the front room again. Instead, she tried to get under the pillow. I could feel her shivering.

"You know Nanny doesn't like you in the bed. Neither

do I. You get your hair all over me when you get up here. Plus your breath stinks."

Thelma let out a sigh of her own.

We Fletchers are a family of sighers.

"Fine," I said, then scooted over some so Thelma could slip into the slight slump in the middle of the bed.

5

Thelma Dog, Part Two

When I woke up the next morning, Thelma had near about pushed me all the way out of the bed. Plus there was a black dog hair in my mouth.

"Geez, girl," I said. She opened an eye at my voice. One of her paws was on my shoulder, the other on my hip like she had meant to snuggle with me or something. Her nose dug in my throat. "You are a bed hog."

Thelma gave me a doggie smile, and I couldn't help but grin right back at her. I got me a soft place in my heart for my own dog. I picked Thelma up at a Sinclair gas station when a guy come driving up, saying he was gonna dump her off in the woods to fend for herself.

I'd left the house that day for cold RC for me and a pack of cigarettes for Nanny and come home with a dog the size of a hoagie.

6

Thelma Dog, Part Three

This here girl is my best friend. Including Patty Bailey.
I never tell Patty that, but Thelma knows the truth.

7
The News

Nanny was at the stove, boiling sugar water to make syrup to go on a new pan of biscuits, when I wandered into the kitchen, Thelma right beside me.

I looked at my grandmother's back. Something wasn't right. I could tell by the way she was hunched over the pot used only for syrup and to make herself that one cup of coffee to start her day. Yes, there was a cup right there, lipstick print on the side. Nanny gets up with the chickens. I mean it. Puts lipstick on then too. Not on the chickens. On herself.

"What's the matter?" I said.

Thelma sat down with a thump and scratched at her collar. It's crocheted. Pink. I made it. Same time I made thirteen doilies (not only pink, all colors), four washcloths, and the beginning of a baby blanket, though I didn't know anyone with a baby. That's why I quit crocheting.

"Let the dog out and we can have us some breakfast and talk."

Thelma looked up at me the way she does when she has to go to the bathroom, her ears back a bit.

"You're scaring me, Nanny." I went through the Florida

room, unlatched the screen door, and watched my best friend slink outside. She'd visit the chickens, I knew, check for critters, and stand at the door when she was ready to come inside.

"You know what the problem is," Nanny said when I got back to the kitchen. She was still standing there, this time with the coffee cup in her hand.

"I don't," I said. It felt like a snake squeezed at my throat.

"The Blue Goose won't make it nowhere. Hardly down to the Piggly Wiggly. We can't go get your momma."

8
My Life

My life has no real disappointments. Nothing exciting about it either. I know what I can expect during the summers because summers are always the same, and here are the facts:

1. Popsicles, if I save up a few dimes from turning in Coke bottles then hoof it to the corner market a half mile away for a grape-juice bar and an *Archie* comic book.
2. Days at the beach, if I hoof it a mile and a half in the other direction. I can swim good past the first breaker. That's one of the places I practice.
3. *General Hospital* and *One Life to Live*, Nanny propped up on the sofa right beside me, tissues within reach.
4. The library and true detective stories and romance novels, as many as I can check out.
5. Busing tables at Leon's restaurant.

I could use a good boyfriend, but I would never tell anyone that.

9
My Momma

Momma left when I was four and she was twenty-one.

Nanny says I was the cutest thing anyone ever did see and that made Momma wish all the more she was a movie star, and the next thing Nanny knew my momma had borrowed her daddy's car (for good), the Lemon, and took off headed west, for California, and for fame.

She sent postcards all the time in the beginning, fewer the more time went on. I've saved them.

Hey Girlies,
Been dancing in Vegas. Thank goodness I got me them tap lessons I wanted when I was little Momma.

Or

How's My Girls,
Done met someone who said I could be a star.

And every once in a while a letter would come like this

Maybe I will come home soon.
Nothing seems to be working my way.

Nanny and me? We have been doing fine. I missed Momma about a year when I was nothing but a baby, but since I have been a-okay. The cards make her more real, and I can imagine her the best person ever, the kind of person Nanny says she was.

Not the kind who would leave her kid.

10

My Momma, Part Two

Nanny says Momma had "a pretty good self-esteem" and was "never really satisfied" being born and raised in New Smyrna Beach, Florida.

"I told her," Nanny has said, "not to leave, and for sure not to leave her little girl with an old woman." (Nanny is in her forties and would look younger, I bet, if she'd lay off the ciggies. All that smoking has made lines appear around her mouth. Her hair, though, is still dark as night with just three white hairs that she won't pull out when I suggest that she do so. "They double. You pull one out, tomorrow you got two where the one was." Instead my grandmother complains about going gray.)

When Nanny tells me stories about my mother, I kind of shrug them off. If anything, I feel sort of blah about her. I don't think of Momma often—except when a postcard comes. Or the dreaded letter. Why should I? She's not here.

She's *never* been here.

Instead, I hide the correspondence in a shoe box under my bed and worry about what's going on with whoever is in love on *General Hospital* or *One Life to Live*. Will I find my own leading man? Or I wonder if I can get a hundred bottles collected for five bucks so I can take me and Nanny to the drive-in and buy us hot dogs.

There's nothing better than a drive-in hot dog.

But the biggest wonder I have is if I will swim in the 1976 Summer Olympics. My most secret goal of all.

11
Momma's Thinking

What would my momma think if she knew I was the fastest-swimming girl in all my high school (both with the backstroke *and* the butterfly)?

What would she think to know I timed myself (with Patty Bailey's help) and have proven I can outswim half the *boys* on the team too?

What would she think if I told her I swim in her old suit, one I found at the bottom of a box of saved items my grandmother has hidden away in case her daughter waltzes herself back home?

12
More of Momma's Thinking

Does *she* have a poster of Mark Spitz on her wall?

Did she spend her hard-earned money on *Sports Illustrated* to get the latest facts on him?

Did she find a way into the school pool, long after the bona fide swimmers are gone, and it's just her and the clock, the lanes marked with blue and white buoys, the sound of life magnified whenever she's under the water?

13
Fool

I am fooling myself.
    My momma thinks nothing at all about me.
    Stolen swimming time or not.

14
Nanny

Nanny would kill me if she knew I broke into the school to swim.

Kill.

I swear. With her bare hands.

I know what she would say while she was doing it. *You could have drowned, and been found floating, hair like a blond sheet, facedown. And how would I feel burying my only granddaughter?*

Some things—like breaking and entering into the high school's facility—are better left unsaid.

15

Nanny, Again

Now Thelma whined at the back door, but I ignored her. Outside, the eaves dripped the leftover rain. Inside, everything felt damp, the way the house always does before and after a good storm.

"What do you think's gonna happen to Momma?" I said.

Nanny didn't say anything, just took little sips of her coffee.

I sighed, making sure I did it all quietlike. "We don't need her here," I said after a minute.

Outside Denny let out a crow that sounded about as breathy as my sigh. That thing is on his last leg. Really. He's a one-legged rooster that Nanny has grown attached to and won't kill 'cause she says he'd make a tough chicken stew, but I know it's because she's fond of him. She bathes him and lets him inside and everything.

Nanny came to the table, a platter of biscuits in one hand and the pot of hot syrup in the other. I smelled vanilla and maple. My stomach growled. Thelma let out a yip by the screen door.

"Go get the hash browns," Nanny said, and I did.

"This day"—Nanny set everything out on hot pads so's not to scar the Formica—"is the day I been waiting on."

I swallowed a glob of spit, then filled my blue plate with biscuits, steaming and buttery. I couldn't split them open fast enough. Piled up those extra-crispy hash browns, too.

"I miss your momma," Nanny said, then bowed her head, just like that, so we could pray.

16
Surprise 2

I felt my eyes grow wide, but I tried to keep control of them.

Nanny missed Momma.

Who'da thunk it?

17

Nanny, Part Three

Nanny hasn't cried one tear of my entire life. She doesn't cry at our soaps—and doesn't look at me when I do.

She didn't shed a tear at *Love Story* when Ryan O'Neal's most beloved Ali MacGraw succumbed to cancer and died in his very arms. I cried so hard that Thelma, who sat in the middle at the drive-in, howled when licking my tears away didn't help. Nanny said, "Love means way more than saying sorry, Winston, and don't you forget it." Then she threw her cigarette out the window, gunned the motor, and drove away, almost tearing the speaker off the pole outside the car.

Nanny didn't shed a tear when Neil Armstrong bounced out of the Apollo 11 capsule saying, "That's one small step for man, one giant leap for mankind." I got teary eyed at that, right there in the classroom.

She didn't even cry when Cassius Clay won his fight against Sonny Liston years earlier. And she had five bucks on that one.

No, my grandmother is fierce as a bear and doesn't have time for tears.

18

Nanny, Part Four

Here are things Nanny *does* have time for:

1. Me
2. Thelma
3. Her job as head cashier and front-end manager at Leon's Seafood Restaurant
4. Denny and the rest of the chickens
5. Watching sports
6. Reading Harlequin romances by the stack from our downtown library
7. Soaps with her best and only granddaughter

19
Worries

I have to say, seeing my nana with her head down like that worried me.

"We can get there somehow," I said. My fingers were sticky, though I used a fork to eat. "If you want. Nevada's not so far from Florida."

Nanny looked up at me. Outside I could hear the chickens waking, letting out soft clucks. They always make these noises that I'm pretty sure mean the day is fresh and new. They got going-to-bed sounds too. I wiped at my forehead, which had gone sweaty with Nanny's glare.

"More'n twenty-three hundred miles," she said.

"Really?"

Nanny nodded. "I checked over with Mr. Wilson."

Mr. Wilson runs the two gas pumps out on the road into town proper. He laughs at everything I say and gives me chunks of sugarcane when we stop to get gas. He doesn't mind if we can only afford thirty-two cents worth of fuel. Maybe everybody in New Smyrna Beach buys that much at a time.

Oh well. I shrugged. But I said the right thing. "It doesn't look so far on the map in Mr. Redfoot's class."

"I know it," Nanny said, and set to eating.

20
Working

Nanny and I ate the rest of breakfast in silence, then I went to gather eggs.

"I got to go to work at eleven," Nanny said. "Check the till and fold up silverware in napkins. You want to bus tables during rush for a bit of cash? Maudy called this morning to say she wouldn't be in. Again."

Maudy's getting ready to marry some navy boy and misses a lot of work.

I'd wanted to stay home and read *The Adventuress*. Her tawny lover would tame her wild desires. Said so on the cover. I wanted to see how the green-eyed vixen got what was coming to her.

Nanny clucked her tongue at me, meaning *Get on with it, girl, make a decision*. She had changed into a pair of black nylon pants and a white shirt. Her hair was held back in a silver clasp, and she wore red lipstick, the only makeup she ever puts on. She doesn't need mascara, not the way her black eyelashes curl up on that tanned skin.

"Depends," I said, gesturing at the T-shirt-no-bra-cutoff-jeans look that is my fashion statement. Quick, like a hummingbird, came this thought: *What's Momma wearing this morning?* The consideration caused me to stumble a little.

"Hurry it up," Nanny said. She'd gathered her pocket-book and now stashed a fresh pack of cigarettes in it. Her low heels clicked on the wooden floor.

"Sorry," I said, gathering my wits. "Can I stay in this? The apron goes to my calves, you know, so I should be okay. People wouldn't see what I'm wearing."

This is what I say every morning before going to work.

Nanny shrugged. "If you contain your womanhood."

That's what Nanny always says too.

I rolled my eyes. Big bosoms run in the family. Nanny can hardly see over hers. At least, that's what she says. She also says I am on my way to what God gave her, whether I like it or not. At this point, I don't care one way or the other. Unless, of course, I can't see what's in front of me. Or these bosoms keep me from the Olympics. I bet it's been known to happen.

"Let's get then," Nanny said, so I let Thelma in, fed her, kissed her three times on the forehead, put on a bra, brushed my teeth, waved good-bye to my Mark Spitz poster, and we got.

21
Nanny's True Love

Leon's is about the onliest place in several cities—including Orlando—with seafood so good that every US president has stopped in for a meal at least once. Richard Nixon came in with a whole bunch of people last December.

I don't know how long ago, Nanny helped her best friend Leon Simmons start the place. A million years ago, maybe? Anyway, I think she hopes he might leave his wife, Janet Green Simmons, and partner up with Nanny for the business *and* for life.

"Last time I cried," Nanny told me once, "was over Leon Simmons."

It was a moment of weakness, the telling.

"I believe you," I had said.

"But your granddaddy was a good man while he lasted, and he cared for me that little while. And now, with him gone, I got all that I need. You and Thelma and Denny." She'd looked off sort of thoughtful. Had she been thinking of my momma then? And I hadn't known it?

Granddaddy took off right after he impregnated my grandmother. But not in his car. He rode away on a Greyhound bus. Denny and Thelma weren't alive at the time.

With all that leaving going on in my young life (and before it too), you might think me bitter or gimpy or maybe a girl with a twitchy eye. That is not the case.

Here's how I see it. There is such a thing as one true love.

Sometimes you marry the wrong man and have the wrong kids but the right granddaughter. Later you get a best dog and a pet rooster, too.

Some people are lucky.

Like Nanny and me.

22
Wishes

Sometimes . . .

Sometimes you wish the man you loved saw you past his long bangs and girlfriends and surfboard.

But that is the way life is.

Maybe some green-eyed vixens are not meant to be tamed. Even if they want taming.

23

My True Love

On our way out to Leon's, the Blue Goose sputtering like he couldn't make it another mile but somehow enduring, I thought about *my* true love. Steve Simmons the First. That's right. Leon and Janet's only son. (He is a very close second on the love meter to Mark Spitz.)

This early afternoon, the car windows were down, even though summer was already so hot I thought I'd melt into a puddle of grease. Dang this bra! I sweated extra every place that thing cinched me.

(Soon as I got the apron on, I would take this bra off, hide it in the walk-in freezer near the fresh-cut beef, and put it on before I left work, so the ride home would be cool and comfortable, at least for a mile or so.)

Here's the scoop. Not about my bra. About Steve Simmons the First.

I have loved Steve since third grade, when I was sure I wouldn't make it home from school and he towed me on his bike to the light at the big road. We separated there, and I walked the rest of the way, stopping only to pee in the ditch where the weeds were high, and I was worried a snake might bite me in the privates.

Anyway.

Steve talked to me in those days. Said things like "hey" when I went to Leon's and he was there.

He said hey to me all the way to sixth grade, when all the sudden girls saw him to be the tall cute guy that he is.

But I've known how great Steve was all along.

Maybe he can't see the real me past my bosoms.

24
Work, Part Two

When I got to work with Nanny, she set to checking the restaurant out, and I set to making sure that the glasses on the tables were all clean, the silverware was folded in the linen napkins, and there wasn't a fly in the place. I mean I did all that after I visited the Deepfreeze.

Leon's is where I took my first step, and truth be told, there is something about owning a restaurant. Or at least working in one that your nanny's friend owns and she *sorta* owns, though I am not sure how it works, seeing they are rich and we collect our eggs from the backyard and not the Piggly Wiggly.

I have another secret wish.

That I can sometime open my own restaurant and make a bundle of money, like the Simmonses have. That will be after my swimming career is over. If Shane Gould can do it this summer, well, why not me? I'll hang my gold medals on the wall over the cash register. And when the place is a roaring success, I will hand the keys over to Nanny and say, "Here you go."

"After lunch rush," Nanny said now, tapping her nails on the countertop, "I need you to go check the plants at the

Simmons place. Make sure they have enough water."

See what I mean about rich? Leon and Janet and Steve the First Simmons have gone off on an adventure. To visit Europe. That's what Leon's hard work has done for them. At least that's what Nanny says. And I believe her. She may be old, but my grandmother knows a lot of stuff. Like how to train a one-legged rooster to walk and how to balance the books of a successful restaurant and how to raise a daughter and then a granddaughter, all on her own.

"I'll do it," I said. Just like that I knew today would be different, sort of like yesterday was with that letter from Momma.

What would make it different? My heart thrummed like when I stand all illegal at the edge of the smooth-watered high school swimming pool.

Today I'd investigate Steve's room.

25

Steve

Last time me and Nanny were in the Simmonses' mansion
(Nanny made me go with her so she wouldn't have to talk
to Janet Green Simmons all alone, which is exactly what
ended up happening because that woman is the bossy type),
I thought about it. You know, how I would go and take a
peek at his door.

Then *he* barreled past in his swimming trunks with
Angel Franklin attached to his hand (she was in a bikini),
to his pool, and he was so tan, and his hair was so blond,
and his momma was yelling at him to get his chores done
and he was ignoring her and Angel was saying, "Is it cold?
Is it cold?" so I never really had the chance to do more than
think, then stare at him and wish that was me in that pink
shimmery two-piece.

No one would have had to throw me in the pool. I
would have dived right in—a perfect slice that wouldn't
even make a splash.

26

Anticipation

My blood felt warmer than normal all during lunch service. My cheeks stayed pink.

I have to say I hate having a crush on a guy.

I wish I could be like Angel. Maybe money makes you fit in better. Maybe it makes you think different.

Maybe that's what Momma thought when she left me and Nanny. That money might somehow save her.

27
Plan

"The Simmonses are gone," I whispered as I filled glasses with ice. I felt like someone from *The Twilight Zone* maybe. Or Victoria Winters from *Dark Shadows*.

They are all in Europe, I thought as I cleaned up a spill in the lobby where Nanny handed out icy glasses of tea and water and lemonade while people waited for their tables to come empty. *I could swim. Eat something from their refrigerator.*

I kept wondering what Steve's room would look like. Would it be stylish and nautical like *McCall's* magazine said was hip? Or all browns and tans the way some other magazines showed was cool. I imagined things so hard I overfilled one customer's water glass and forgot to top off another person's unsweetened tea.

"I'll even look in his drawers," I said as I took all the dishes from table eighteen, where a family had eaten more crab claws than should be allowed.

"Where's your bra?" Nanny said as I passed close enough for her to get a good look.

"Cooling off," I said and hurried away, the tub laden with dirty platters and bowls and silverware, and then to the freezer so I could be prepared when Nanny and I met up again.

28

Preparing for the Plan

The Simmons house was quiet and cool. And huge. Huge! It would take me an hour to check all the plants. I know because I've done this with Nanny before. Janet Green Simmons is too busy to water her own plants. She has things to do.

I set the key on the table after I let myself in the grand foyer and went out to the garage to get the watering can. I came back through the kitchen that I know they never cook in and that I know Nanny would love to get her hands dirty in. I would water plants in the dining room first.

Here there are windows that look out at the pool, and past that the lawn and all the way down to the shoreline of the Atlantic Ocean. From where I stood, I could hear the crash of the waves. Thelma would love this house. So would Denny. And Nanny.

I sighed.

"Get to work," I said to myself.

My hands already ached from carrying that tub full of dishes back and forth to Raul, who washed them fast as he could for the next rush of people, and I was dirty now even though I wore an apron all during service. Somehow I'd gotten chicken-fried-steak gravy in my hair. Busing is hard business.

"First things first," I said, and took off my bra and stuck it in the freezer next to the Borden's cherry vanilla ice cream. Then I started watering.

And watering.

And watering.

29

The Olympics

I looked at the Simmonses' pool.

It seemed extra long. I bet our Olympic athletes could practice in that thing.

What did a three-person family need with a pool this size so close to the ocean? They could step into the surf from their front door. Well. Almost.

"Do it." I whispered the words, fogging up the bit of glass. Running my fingers through my breath, I answered myself, "Are you crazy? No. Way."

There's no one here.

Good grief. I knew that. Wasn't I watering and dusting and peeping in drawers to see what all was in this place? Didn't I plan to look in Steve's room today? This very day? I knew I was alone. I didn't need to convince me of anything.

I rubbed at my arms. Why in the world had the Simmonses left the air conditioning on? Did their precious plants need to be cool? Disgusting.

I went back to the ferns and peace lilies and moth orchids, checking the dirt with my thumb, passing by the ones that shouldn't be watered at all.

Even their plants bloomed while they were gone.

What would Janet Green Simmons do if I overwatered?

Underwatered?

Water.

The pool.

Go.

30
Temptation

The plants on the main floor (which was as big as the Piggly Wiggly, if you ask me) were done.

I wandered to the fridge.

It was about empty. Beer. Bologna. Milk. *That* would go bad in almost three months.

So what? Let them come home to cheese. And bologna bricks.

"That's it," I said into the fridge, which was about as cold as the kitchen felt. Stinkin' fridge was big enough to sleep in.

I closed my eyes and shut the door, then turned around and leaned on the counter. What was the matter with me? Why was I mad? I don't ever get mad.

They had a pool.

Sure.

They were rich because of Leon's.

Sure.

Me and Nanny weren't.

Sure.

Steve could practice for the Olympics, but he played football instead.

Go.

"That's it," I said. "I'm gonna do it."

31
Doing It Once

I walked fast before I could change my mind.

Out the french doors.

Onto the back porch that was big enough to park cars on.

I slipped off my shorts.

Kicked off my flip-flops. Placed my T-shirt on top of everything as though I offered a gift to the swimming gods.

Were there swimming gods?

Did it matter?

My T-shirt had faded blue and got all stretched out around the neck like I like them. It looked like a jewel there on the white marble of the pool surround.

Should I go back in the house and get my bra? Should I swim in it?

I didn't give myself a chance to answer, just dove into the pool, buck nekkid except my panties. And like that, I was home.

32

Home

Swimming and me.

In a stolen pool, Simmons or high school.

In the ocean.

In Crystal Lake—minus the water moccasins.

Let me swim, I thought, and I worked my way back and forth over that water, going as fast or as slow as I wanted.

Lost track of time.

Of Nanny.

Of Momma's worrisome note.

This was the life. A pool right here. The ocean a few steps beyond.

After a bit I rolled onto my back.

The sun had moved a good deal, but I didn't let that stop me from me from doing what came as natural to me as walking or running did.

Instead I planned. I'd go inside quick, take care of the plants upstairs, catch a glimpse or two of Steve's room, then jog back to Nanny, who I bet had chewed her fingernails to the quick by now, worrying.

I blew a spout of water into the air.

Sure. I'd do that soon.

33

Executing the Plan, Plus Surprise 3

It was a mess. And smelled like burning oak leaves.

When I pushed the door open and saw his bedroom, I couldn't believe it looked this way. Nanny would have my hide if I left things piled all over the floor, dishes on the dresser, the bed unmade.

Now I took a step, over a tangle of blue jeans, a skateboard, and underwear turned inside out. Nerves thumped through my veins and I swallowed. There was a mirror I could sort of see myself in, covered by more posters and pictures of girls from school. I recognized Angel and a girl named Whitney and the twins Samantha and Sabrina. Why were they hugging like that?

Posters of Led Zeppelin, Aerosmith, and Alice Cooper covered one wall. There were several lava lamps, all going, blobs of lava (what was that stuff? I wasn't sure, but I wanted one) floated to the top of the bulb-thing then settled back down.

Steve Simmons the First couldn't have been further from *McCall's* than I was with my one Mark Spitz poster.

"I could live like this," I whispered. "I could get used to it. Marry him. Have his babies." I cleared my throat. "After the Olympics of course." For a moment I imagined myself picking up after Steve.

Maybe no to the babies.

Another step.

There on the floor was a stack of *Playboy*s. One was open and . . . I looked away from the topless girl. Were . . . were these magazines Steve's? They couldn't be. They must be his father's, and his father came in this room to read them—or look at them—or whatever you did with a *Playboy*, so his wife wouldn't know.

What would Nanny think of this?

And couldn't those lava lamps, plugged in and going for three months straight, couldn't that cause a fire or something?

34

Surprise 4

"What are you doing in here?"

My hand shook so hard that water from the watering can slopped over the sides and landed on Steve's underwear. I opened and closed my mouth three times, like an old catfish on a line. I felt as trapped. I wanted to run. To dive from his balcony and into the pool. I wanted to turn and stare into his face, but I couldn't quite move.

Steve Simmons was here. Now. In this room. Here.

Now.

Not in Europe at all.

Here.

I almost dropped the watering can. I found my tongue, hidden in the back corner of my mouth. "What am *I* doing in here? What are *you* doing in here? That's the real question."

Steve cocked his head at me, birdlike. "I live here."

"Uh."

He was right about that.

"You're *supposed* to be in France or something."

Steve pushed past me and into his the-bomb-just-went-off room. "Didn't go," he said.

That was obvious.

He turned and eyed me. "Watched you swimming," he said.

Something inside my gut burst into flames.

"You saw—saw me?" I crossed my arms in front of my chest.

Steve pulled his shirt off and threw it on one of the piles in front of a walk-in closet that was bigger than our living room. He didn't say anything.

"You spied," I said. My face felt steamy. Maybe through this smoky haze he couldn't see. Wait. Why was it smoky in here? "I think that's against the law. Spying."

Maybe he couldn't see the wet imprints of my breasts or the water slipping down my legs. I should have used a real towel to dry off on, not that fancy thing I found in the kitchen sink.

"Winston Churchill," Steve said, his voice smoky as the room. "You were in *my* pool. How's that for breaking the law?"

I looked away. Breaking and entering into a private pool. Wouldn't look good on my record.

Thank goodness I hadn't made that bologna sandwich.

"Fine," I said, and turned away.

"Why're you in here, anyway?"

I raised the watering can, which wasn't easy seeing my own arms had a tight grip on my body. "Watering. I'm watering. Plants." The words came out like a bit of wind. I saw my mouth move in the section of uncovered mirror. Steve is so tall I couldn't see his face in the glass. Ozzy Osbourne's head was where Steve's chest should be instead.

He moved past me (not Ozzy, Steve) toward a drawer, where he pulled out another T-shirt, brushing my elbow. It felt like a bee might have stung where we touched. He put on the shirt, then took a sort of leap and landed on his back on the bed. Water sloshed this way and that. Blood rushed to my head and for a moment I felt dizzy. I looked back at Ozzy.

"There are no plants in here," he said, "unless you count this." He opened his bedside table drawer and took out a rolled cigarette. Nanny's brother, Uncle Buddy, coulda taught Steve a thing or two about rolling something to smoke. "Just a little weed."

"Weed?" I gripped the handle of the can so hard my knuckles felt like they might snap like chicken bones.

Steve laughed. "Want to smoke with me?"

Wait a minute.

That's why there was all this smoke.

And wait another minute.

I knew . . . I knew what he was talking about. Drugs. Without an answer, I turned and left, left the whole house. Down the long staircase, through that massive foyer, and out the front door.

Past the garages, past a brand-new motor home that looked bigger than our place, up that driveway that seemed to grow longer and longer like something from *Alice in Wonderland*.

What in the world were the Simmonses doing leaving a pretty boy like Steve here, alone? It was obvious he needed help cleaning his room. And that he had a severe, severe problem with illegal drugs.

35

Surprise 5

"Where you going, Churchill?"

"Don't call me that."

Steve beat me to the end of the driveway. Well, he knew the house better than I did. So? So? Sew buttons on your underwear.

Were there buttons on his underwear?

I couldn't bear to think about it in the broad light of day. I'd have to save underwear-button thinking for later on tonight when no one would see my face color in the late afternoon air.

I marched back toward Leon's, with a half-ish mile to go. My ponytail jumped in the breeze. Thank goodness we were so close to the ocean. The smell cleared my head. I wanted to march harder, move faster, but I could only go so quick because of my freed bosoms. It's hard to book it when you have your arms folded across your chest.

Wait. Wait.

No!

Steve cut in front of me and walked backward.

"I said, where you off to?"

I didn't look at him. But my mouth went on its own.

"No you didn't," I said, staring straight ahead. "You said, where you going."

"Churchill," he said.

"What?" I pretended to look at him by glancing at a palmetto tree off behind Steve's shoulder across the street.

My bra. Oh, my bra. Nanny warned me about putting it in the freezer, but I never listen.

Now I couldn't think.

"I said your name, too," he said, and his voice was so sweet I had to look him in the eyes. Eyes blue as the ocean. He almost smiled. We both stopped walking.

"That's not my name. It's Winston."

"I know that," Steve said. "Winston *Churchill*."

I rolled my eyes.

"Why're you carrying that watering can?"

What? That too? "Uh."

"Here. I can take care of it."

"No," I said, but he wrestled it from my hand.

It was only half-full of water. Somehow I had slopped the rest down my leg. I noticed, for the first time, my flip-flop was wet.

"I can take that back," I whispered.

"Naw," Steve said, then threw the can high over a coquina-rock wall and into another rich person's yard. He took a step closer to me, and I tightened my arms over my bosoms. He was so pretty I couldn't stand it. We stood there close enough that if I had crept forward even a bit more, we would have been touching.

A Volkswagen roared past, stopped short, and snaked back to where Steve and I gazed at each other. The car went up on the sidewalk, and Benjy Aufhammer stuck his head out the window.

Ick.

More football players. Too many crammed in a Volkswagen. If I hadn't been so horrified to be caught out on the street in dirty clothes, with gravy in my hair (or had the pool water washed it out?), my bra in a stranger's freezer, and with the boy I was in love with, I would have smiled at Steve *and* at Benjy, but my lips were as frozen as some of my apparel was.

"Simmons, let's go," Benjy Aufhammer said. "We done stopped at your place and you weren't there."

Smart, I wanted to say, but I kept quiet.

Someone let out a whistle from the backseat, and someone else said, "Dammit, Creed. There's too many of us in here for you to be doing that. Now I'm deaf."

Benjy revved the motor.

And just like that Steve Simmons, the boy of my dreams, kissed me full on the lips.

36
Taming

The biggest, longest, most taming kiss ever.

37
Boys

Somebody laughed as I let my hands flop like two eels at my side. I touched a bit of fabric from his shirt.

Steve pulled away and looked me hard in the face when the smooch was over. I thought I might end up a puddle of melted butter on the sidewalk.

"See ya," he said. His voice was low. So soft I might have made up even hearing it. Steve ran around the car, looked at me over the top of the Bug, then slid in through the passenger window.

Benjy drove off, leaving black tread marks on the concrete, Steve's legs dangling out the window from the knees on down.

I wiped at my lips, a weak protest on my tongue.

I blinked.

That was the sweetest kiss I'd ever gotten. The only kiss, yes. But the sweetest, too. Did the weed make Steve taste like that? Like milk chocolate? Or was this his natural taste? Did all boys taste so sweet?

What had I tasted like? Gravy? Scallops? The bit of orange lip gloss I had applied this morning?

Did he care?

Would he kiss me again?

I stood there on the sidewalk, watching that car till it wasn't the size of a postage stamp, then I walked all the way back to work, my stomach flopping over itself till I felt sick.

38

Stuck

No watering can, no key, no bra.

A frozen solid bra, truth be told, but not with me.

Now what?

39

New Plans Needed

I wasn't even sure how I made it back to Leon's.

But when I walked in the restaurant, Nanny stopped what she was doing and said, "What happened to you?"

"Nothing," I said. I felt my whole body turning red from the forehead down. Was my chest blotchy? My bosoms obvious? I knew my hair was pool-straggles even pulled back in the ponytail.

There was only one table of customers. I touched my lips.

I thought Nanny would jump over the bar, where she counted glasses for this evening's shift. "I said what happened?"

Raul looked out through the kitchen door.

The restaurant grew as quiet as a church.

"Nothing," I said, and headed to the freezer, where I rubbed crushed ice all over my face till I cooled off.

40
Found Out, Sort Of

"Who kissed you?" Nanny said, first thing, when we climbed into the Blue Goose. "Did you leave your bra in the freezer again?"

My stomach fell into my lap. She didn't need details.

"Yes," I said. "To the bra part." I stared out the window, knowing she would read the lie in my eyes if I looked at her straight in the face. "Why would anyone kiss me, Nanny? People don't even talk to me during the summer. Patty Bailey is gone, you know."

Nanny's voice went low.

"I know that look," she said. "I seen it on your momma's face and I saw it plenty on my own. You cannot fool me."

I turned to my grandmother, pulling in all the fresh ocean air that I could. I looked at her, staring her in the eyes. "I swear to you, Nanny, I haven't kissed anyone at all." That was the truth. I hadn't laid my lips on Steve. He had caught me.

I coulda kept talking. I coulda said, *And I don't ever plan to kiss anyone, not the whole of my life.* But the truth was all that had changed, and I knew, just knew, if Steve Simmons the First was involved, I would be a kissing fool all the rest of my life.

With or without my frozen bra.

41

Surprise 6

Thelma waited for us at the front door, grinning from ear to ear.

"Girl," I whispered, kneeling close and hugging her neck. She had that perfect doggie smell if I avoided her breath. "I got so much to tell you."

Nanny looked at me from across the front porch, where she dug the mail out of the box then sorted it. She paused.

"What?" I said.

"Another letter," Nanny said. Nanny waved it to me, like she wasn't sure if she was happy or sad.

Not a postcard.

A letter.

A letter.

42

How a Life Turns from Sort of Uncomplicated to Very Messed Up

That night, Thelma in the doorway because there was no storm, I lay in bed and stared at the ceiling. Momma's second letter nestled under my pillow, folded perfect, lying right next to the first one.

There was no reason to read it again.

I knew what it said.

Mommy, baby Winston,
   Come git me,
   Please.
   Signed,
   Skye Harper

43
One Problem Solved

I decided, if anyone asked, that it wasn't my bra hiding out in a rich man's house. No one could prove it. And like that, I fell asleep.

44
More Dreams

There was Momma again.

She looked like me, only she was clean and could dance. "I paid for my own tap-dance lessons," she said. She tapped the whole time she talked. And she never got winded, even though she held watering cans in both hands.

45

Surprise 7

"Hey. Hey. Wake up," Momma said, all deeplike. *Tap tap tappity tap.*

I awoke with a start, sitting straight up in bed, my stomach clogging the back of my throat.

The dream had been so real I could hear her voice. I could see Momma's hair, long and blond, like my own. She had dream-danced faster than Shirley Temple and Ann Miller, both Nanny's favorites.

I settled back onto my pillow, covering a yawn. The night light in the hall spilled a bit of cream into my room. Thelma was a black blob.

"Churchill."

Looking toward the window, I saw her. Wait. Here. How? The Lemon was gone. Sold. Momma said so in her first letter. And her voice. Her voice was deep. Like a guy's. What had happened? I squinched my eyes tight, then opened them wide.

"You awake, Churchill? I'm holding on by my fingernails. Come to the window. I got something for you."

That wasn't Momma.

"Steve?" I almost swallowed my tongue. "What in the

world?" I pulled the sheet up to my chin. A bit of Steve's head showed through the screen. The fan took up the rest of the space. "What are you doing here?"

"Visiting," he said.

"What for?"

Light, thin and watery as early morning can be, pushed in around him. Thelma edged into my room some. I could see her eyes were open. Why didn't she bark? Alert me? Protect me? Why, I could be fighting for my virtue right now.

Steve let out a laugh, not too loud, and I was surprised at how deep it sounded.

"To talk. Let me in."

He was crazy. Nanny would jerk a knot in his tail.

"No," I said. "I don't think so."

"Come on," he said, his voice urgent. "I've been thinking about that kiss all night."

Now I hesitated. *I* had been thinking about that kiss too.

"Let me inside."

I sat up, shaking my head. "Go away," I said. "You are in dangerous territory."

"Come out onto the porch then. Your grandmother won't care. I'll wait for you."

Then he was gone.

46

A Meeting Almost Under
the Cover of Darkness

I flopped back in bed, wanting to smile but knowing better. Nanny might know, somehow, I was feeling happy and wake up, then come check on me and force the previous day out of my mouth.

She would so care about the whole thing.

Boys at the window. Bras in their freezers. No, that would not be something that Nanny would approve.

I threw the sheet off, kicked it across the room, slipped on shorts and a fresh T-shirt, and ran, light-footed, across the room, down the hall, and into the living room. I peeked through the front window.

Steve sat in our Adirondack chair, my bra dangling from two fingers, like he was an ad for Sears and Roebuck.

47

Different

He swung that ol' thing around when I stepped onto the porch, Thelma close on my heels.

"Stay," I said to her, closing my best friend in the house, and to Steve I said, "Give me that," and leaped down the stairs, hip-hopping my way to where he sat when I caught a pebble under my heel.

He grinned and got to his feet faster than I thought possible. "Why should I?"

I planted my hands on hips. "Are you kidding? What do you mean, why should you? You should because that's my underwear."

In the gray light of morning, I could see my under-clothing looked a little shabby. Did it smell like cherry vanilla ice cream? Sweat? Thelma?

"You're different," Steve said, and handed the bra to me like his finger was a hook.

"Pardon me?" I wasn't sure what to do with the article of clothing, so I hung the bra on the door knob. Thelma looked out the living room window, paws on the sill. Her nose was pressed to the screen.

Steve shrugged then sat back down. He looked so, I

don't know, at home. So . . . pretty. Something in my heart twisted. I was glad for the pale light. I didn't want him to see that I loved him. Could he tell? If he looked hard enough, could he tell?

"Other girls would have screamed and chased me and made me hold that over my head so they could get it back."

"I see," I said, nodding. "Do you want me to do that? Chase you?" I thought of Angel not diving into the pool on her own. Was there something wrong with me? Something a momma could have bred into me that a grandmother had not?

"No. This is good," Steve said. "You being you." He leaned forward then patted the chair next to him. "We can talk maybe?" He licked his lips, and without meaning to, I started to lick my own. Then stopped. Was that normal? Un-normal?

"For a minute," I said, after considering. "My nanny may not appreciate early-morning visitors." I sat on the other Adirondack, my butt on the edge of the wood. "You be ready to run if I say so."

Steve gave me a bit of a nod. "Okay," he said.

48

Will the Surprises Never Stop?

The sun rose and we talked.

Past chickens getting up, we talked.

Past Thelma wanting to go out, we talked.

We talked all the way till Nanny came out on the front porch and handed us both *handmade* biscuits made into sandwiches with fried ham, surprising all three of us, I think.

"Steve," she said, handing us both a glass of milk, too. "I thought I heard you. You look like your daddy. Except for the hair."

"Thank you, Miss Jimmie," Steve said, and I could see he'd talked to her more than he ever had to me. Before today, I mean. At work, maybe? "I love these biscuits of yours."

Nanny nodded. "I remember." She grabbed up my bra then gave me the evil eye. She slipped back inside, peeking back only once over Thelma, who still watched us, a long bit of drool dangling from her black lips.

49
Nothing

He didn't kiss me good-bye.

50

Nothing at All

Man, I wanted him to.

   Bad.

51
Truths?

"We're leaving," Nanny said when I came inside. Then, "Don't you get too used to that boy. You know his daddy is a heartbreaker. I bet that runs in the genes."

I didn't answer.

"The next time he comes to visit you before the rise of the sun, I'm gonna skin both your hides. Especially if I find you underclothed again."

I flopped next to Nanny where she sat with her crossword puzzle and a steaming cup of coffee. No lipstick print. She must not be going into Leon's today. At least not the morning shift.

"No you won't," I said. "I can see you like him."

Nanny pointed at me with her pen. She always does crossword puzzles in ink. If a word doesn't fit, she makes it. She finishes every puzzle. "I know young crushes," Nanny said. "We Fletchers are notorious for young crushes. I been there. I know what it feels like. *And* I know where it could end up."

I raised my eyebrows.

She let out a sigh. (A sigh!) "I have to tell you, I was pretty surprised to see him on my front porch."

I lowered my eyebrows.

Nanny put the paper away and tucked the pen behind her ear. "Those Simmons boys are charmers," she said. She was almost smiling, looking sort of guilty. "But they got their troubles and all the good looks in the world can't fix that."

Outside, Denny crowed three times, one after the other. He always does, rain or shine, at nine thirty in the morning.

"We got troubles," I said. Only not too loud.

"What's that?" Nanny moved close enough I could smell her coffee breath.

"We got our own troubles, Nanny, and we aren't good-looking like they are." I stared at the built-in bookcase next to the fireplace. There were rows and rows of Reader's Digest books. I'd read all of them, twice.

Now Nanny raised *her* eyebrows. "I beg to differ," she said. She gestured at a photo of Momma, one she sent a couple of years back for Christmas, that Nanny hung over the television. I might be mad at her, but my momma is beautiful. "You get your gorgeous looks from a long line of Southern women."

"Sure." I tried not to sigh.

"Don't sass me now."

I pulled my knees up and wrapped my arms around them. "I'm not."

"Your blond hair with all those curls, the green eyes and"—she paused—"attributes? From me." Nanny waved at the picture.

"You got black hair," I said.

Nanny ignored my comment. "Little bones, small feet, nice eyebrows? From your father's mother."

"Who?"

"We don't speak about her." Nanny got up and went to the back door. "Denny," she called. She stood waiting, but the waiting didn't stop her talking none. "You don't see your good looks 'cause you don't brush your hair gazing in the mirror, do you?"

Again, I didn't answer. How did she know?

"You got that from me too. The me from long ago. You wear the same clothes till the fronts are stained and the back has butt prints from sitting on the ground. Your momma did the same thing. Trust me on this one. That boy was your first kiss 'cause you are beautiful, Winston."

She knew. She knew Steve had kissed me. How? How?

Denny hopped into the house, fluttering his wings a bit as he went, then settled in a little blanket right next to the sofa and in front of the TV so he could watch all our shows with us. Nanny settled beside him to pet his head with her pointer finger.

"I do wonder what that boy is doing home. I thought he was off to Europe with his daddy and momma. Sure does make life more difficult." Nanny stared me down. "Don't you help with that."

"No, ma'am," I said, though I had no idea what she meant.

52

The List

"Start packing," Nanny said, cigarette dangling from her lips. I'd walked her to the car so she could head off to Leon's for the evening shift. The Blue Goose rattled like it needed to shake loose extra parts. Thelma stood on one side of me, panting her good-bye, Denny on the other, balancing pretty good in a stiff breeze that meant a storm was coming. "Keep it light."

"Nanny—" I said, but she interrupted me.

"Don't argue. Get up a few cans of dog food, some non-perishables for us, a bag of corn for Denny. The small one. His traveling cage, plenty of newspapers. I expect we'll be gone two weeks."

Nanny flicked her cigarette, picked tobacco off her tongue, and shifted the Blue Goose into reverse. The car let out a whine that caused Thelma to tilt her head to one side. The left. Like always.

"I don't understand. This ol' thing won't do us a bit of good. We have to pray just so it gets us to and from work."

Nanny backed up, and I walked beside the car as it seemed to cry out in pain. She stopped with a good stomp to the brakes. "I'm going to get my daughter, Winston. Like

I would go after you, if you needed it. Which you never will because you are smarter than Judith Lee."

"But . . ."

"A few changes of clothes, Winston, we won't have a lot of room. Maybe your bathing suit. I know you can't leave that behind. Talk to Wilbur about feeding the hens." She shifted into drive and the Blue Goose made a jump forward, sputtered, and almost died.

A burst of wind blew past, and Denny fluttered around before settling on his one good foot.

"Don't forget their leashes."

Then Nanny was gone, heading down East Lake Drive.

"What is she thinking, Thelma?"

Thelma looked me in the eyes. She smiled. I rubbed at the white marking on her chest. Ran my fingers under her collar.

"She's up to something," I said, and the three of us went into the house.

53
Packing

The storm broke right after I talked to Wilbur, who scrubbed his hand over his face and said, "*You* two going somewhere?" Like that had never happened in our lives. 'Cause it hadn't. "Sure I'll take the eggs in trade of feeding them hens."

Quick, I had to close the windows because rain sprayed in on every side of the house, like we were in a blender or something.

Then I set to gathering everything Nanny had told me to, Thelma so close she kept running into me. She's a chicken when it comes to lightning and thunder. Even Denny is less chicken than our dog when it comes to storms.

When I went into Nanny's room, I found her little packed bag on her made bed.

"Nanny, what is in that head of yours?" I said. I felt a little sick to my stomach.

I turned to leave the room, but something caught my eye. On Nanny's dresser, next to her red lipstick.

My cigar box of postcards and letters from Momma.

54
Payback

What was *that* doing in here? When had Nanny snuck in my room and gotten it?

I closed my eyes a moment.

Imagined Nanny here at the mirror, putting on lipstick (not that she needs a mirror—she can do it with her eyes closed), these few letters right where she could see them.

Did she read them as many times as I had?

She must *really* miss my momma.

I swallowed, nervous. This meant one thing. Looking at those letters, I knew I had to do what Nanny wanted, because she had always, *always*, done for me.

55
Reading Material

So.

I'd have to take a few books. I could stow them under the front seat.

I went to my bookshelf and pulled off *Love's Savage Hot Love*, *The Princess of His Heart*, and *Indian Lover*. I set them in a stack.

Thunder clapped. That's early September for you. Noisy with fall storms.

Thelma tried to crawl in my lap, scraping my leg with her nails.

"Let me see the books, Thelma," I said, working around her trembling body. "It's okay, girl. It'll be over soon."

My Forbidden, *Intertwined*, and *Roses Forever, My Love* were added to the pile.

One more.

Under a Moon So Fine.

There. Something to do when I wasn't helping Nanny drive.

56

For Nanny

I woke to Nanny speaking in my ear.

"We gotta get a move on, Winston. Weather's cleared. You ready?"

No. No I wasn't ready to go off. I kept my eyes closed. I wanted to stay here. Where Steve was, in case he visited again in the middle of the night. Or wanted to kiss me by the ocean. Or in his room. I wanted to be able to walk to the beach and swim. Or smuggle myself into the school pool so I could practice.

Plus, I liked being a part of this little family that was missing a mother. And tell me this—why should Momma get to run off anytime she wanted and then come home when she wanted? It wasn't—

"Winston?"

"I'm ready," I said, and tossed the sheet off.

I was doing this for my grandmother. All I had to do was remember that.

"Make your bed, sweets, we are off on an adventure."

57
Remembrances

When I stepped outside, the earth wet and dripping, I couldn't quite focus my eyes. I mean, I wasn't seeing things right. I was in a dream world.

Dreaming.

Again.

I pinched my arm then looked to Nanny and back at the driveway again.

"Don't say anything," Nanny said. "I packed us up. Go on and get in."

"But ..."

"But nothing," Nanny said.

Late morning fog settled on the yard, the neighborhood, skimming Wilbur's roof.

"But ..."

Nanny stopped by the U-shaped driveway, the Blue Goose looking shiny in the porch light's reflection. She turned to me. "I know you don't understand any of this, Winston, but I got to go get my girl."

Nanny, who never talks in a low voice, not even in church, almost whispered when she spoke. "I begged her not to go. And she went anyway. I promised myself I'd do my best to get her back if she ever needed me. It's been a decade without a visit." Nanny walked over to me and took hold of my shoulders. "You need to know your mother, Winston, and all that's good about her. I need to hug her one more time."

I dropped my head and after a moment, looked up at my grandmother. "Okay," I whispered back. Then I went to the Simmonses' brand-new motor home (the talk of the town), opened the door, and climbed on in.

58
And So It Begins

I felt like I sat on top of a school bus, only the ride was way more comfortable.

"I bet this uses a lot of gas," I said when Nanny and I were headed up I-95 toward Jacksonville.

Nanny was pitched forward in her chair, looking like she was ready to wrestle a bear.

"Relax," I said.

"Can't," Nanny said. "Get me a cigarette."

"What?"

Nanny hit a pothole and dishes rattled. I bounced in my seat. Thelma let out a nervous moan. I couldn't see her that well, tucked up under the table the way she was. Only the glitter of her eyes. Denny didn't make a sound. He's used to riding around with Nanny. He's used to the potholes.

"I said get me a cigarette. I'm nervous as hell."

Soon as it was broad daylight, I thought, getting the pack for my grandmother, I would check out the motor home, see what all it contained. Why, if we weren't being felons right now this would have been fun.

Come on, truth be told, it was a *little* fun—being all perched up here like the Queen of the Night, or something.

I shook my head. "I don't think so," I said, putting the cigarettes in the glove compartment. "We can't steal someone's motor home and then smell it up with these stinky things. You're gonna have to smoke only at rest stops."

Nanny gave me the old evil eye.

"You better watch the road," I said. "You want to wreck a stolen vehicle?"

Nanny didn't say a thing.

59

Breaking the Bank

In St. Augustine we stopped at the Publix to get lunch and fill the fridge.

"We're not too far from the fort," I said when we pulled into the parking lot.

Nanny gave me a little nod. "We can't stop," she said. "Only for gas and food and to stretch our legs. I'm going to see what I can do to stay up and drive all night."

What? All night? Not sleeping till Vegas? I couldn't look at my grandmother.

We hurried into the grocery store. The air was cool and smelled like bread.

"Wait," I said, stopping right by the newspaper stand that displayed pictures of Germany and the Olympics. "We gotta sleep."

There he was, Mark Spitz, on the cover of *Sports Illustrated*. I pulled the magazine off the display case. Held it to my chest.

"You can get that," Nanny said. "Put it in the cart."

"Really?"

"And listen. I been thinking. You can drive late evenings when the roads are less busy." My grandmother hurried down the aisle. "I can take catnaps. I'll drink a lot of coffee. We could make it in record time. Three days tops."

Nanny grabbed me by the sleeve and pulled me in front of the fruits and vegetables. She loaded up a cart, even grabbing dry cereal (something we never buy) and milk.

Ahead of us, a mother with five little girls tried to pick out a cantaloupe.

"Wait a minute," I said, and touched Nanny's arm. Her skin was soft under my fingertips and warm as a match. Being a felon didn't seem to set well with her. "Nanny, how we paying for all this?" I clutched the magazine, ready to put it back.

She swallowed. "I emptied our account." Nanny pushed ahead, now piling yogurt into the cart.

"We've only got one hundred and eighty dollars," I said. "I know that for a fact."

She looked at me long and hard. "Winston," she said. "I got us covered. Promise. We have enough to get to where we are going and back. You got to trust me."

"Okay," I said, and when my stomach settled some, I picked out a dozen doughnuts. 'Cause Nanny said I could.

60
Stocking Up

I walked Thelma on a bit of grass, gave her something to eat and drink while Nanny did the same for Denny, leading him under a tree on his crocheted leash.

"Like your chicken," a cute guy with black hair said. He held tight to his girlfriend, who laughed behind her hand. She wore short-shorts and reminded me of Angel. Were all girls the same? All but me? What was Steve Simmons the First doing right now? Did he notice his motor home was missing? Had he called the police?

"Thank you, but it's a rooster," Nanny said, drawing deep on her cigarette. She was trying to get three smokes into the one stop. "We're having him for dinner."

The couple hurried on.

I'd already used the restroom in Publix (where shopping really was a pleasure, and we got a lot of S&H Green Stamps to boot), washing my face and et cetera.

"Let's get a move on," Nanny said. "We shouldn't have to stop again except to gas up."

I still couldn't quite look at her. Not full on. I'd never really thought she was a full-blown thief, but proof was twenty-five feet behind me. And I had a sneaking suspicion she wasn't telling all about our funds, though in my whole life my nanny had never been anything but 100 percent honest. The one time I took Wilbur's blackberries from his bushes (I was five), she made me confess then wash his dishes three nights in a row. I cried the whole time, going over the single plate, glass, and fork as she stood behind me saying, "You missed a spot."

Now, as I climbed into the motor home, I wondered what Nanny's punishment would be. More than washing a few dishes, that was for sure.

The thought made me light-headed.

61

Checking the Rig Out

I ate three doughnuts (one raspberry jelly, one bavarian cream, and a glazed), sharing bits with Thelma, who rested her head on my lap.

Nanny drove like she expected a tidal wave to wash us away, both hands on the steering wheel, a look of concentration that I am sure Superman uses to blast holes through steel doors.

"I'm gonna wash my hands," I said, licking icing from my fingers, "and see what this place is all about."

Nanny grunted.

"Don't you bet it cost a million dollars?"

This time Nanny didn't say anything. She would have a crick in her neck, sure, if she didn't loosen up some.

I stepped over Denny's cage, giving him a few bits of doughnut to enjoy, then walked to the sink.

This motor home was nicer than our house. The carpet was new and thick. The plaid sofa didn't even look used. Maybe the Simmonses never went anywhere in this thing.

There was a bed above us. Cool! And then a table, with benches (same plaid cushions as the sofa) built into the floor. A bed over the front seats. A fridge. The countertop was a shiny new yellow (harvest gold, if you're looking for technical terms), and there was a stainless-steel sink, a big one, considering. There was a stove top and even a microwave. A microwave! I've been asking Nanny to buy us one of those for ages, but she was all worried about radiation waves getting out of the machine and cooking us from the inside out.

"You wanna die from a terrible poisoning?" That's what she asked me the last time I begged for an Amana.

"Not really," I'd said.

"It's a terrible way to go. We're using the stove top and oven only. You'll thank me later."

Now I opened the microwave.

First thing I was doing was cooking something—I didn't know what—in this here fancy-schmancy device. The thing made me smile.

All the cabinets were empty of food, so I pulled the groceries from the bags and put them away, the milk and yogurt and cheese into the small fridge, then locked everything shut. I could get used to the rumble of the road beneath my feet.

Thelma swayed beside me, trying to keep her footing. She had her side glued to my leg. She's a pretty good traveler, that dog.

I stepped down the hall. One two three.

A shower there. A mirror. The toilet. I sat on it after pulling some TP off the roll and laying it across the seat.

Across the way was a closet. I'd keep my clothes in my Piggly Wiggly grocery bag. The idea of using the Simmonses' coat hangers—it seemed too personal. Wasn't the toilet seat enough?

I slid the back curtain open.

Steve Simmons grinned at me from the huge bed. "I wondered when you would find me back here," he said.

62
Huh?

I couldn't move.

63
Will Wonders Never Cease?

"What?"

I stood there, curtain in hand, swaying back and forth. Thelma cocked her head from side to side and grinned. She jumped on the bed and padded right up next to Steve then plopped down on the unmade bed beside him.

Geezo peazo. Nanny was gonna . . .

She was gonna crap a brick.

What was *he* doing here? I couldn't feel my feet. I felt like I do whenever I swim too long. Light-headed and footless. Neither is a good sensation when swimming or when standing in the back of a million-dollar motor home looking at the cutest boy in all of New Smyrna Beach, Florida.

"I said, what are you doing here?" I whispered, and gestured one-handed just in case he couldn't hear me over the highway flying behind us.

"No you didn't." Steve gave me a slow smile.

Had I thought those words? Was I losing my speaking ability, too?

"Okay, then. What are you doing here?" The words came out from between clenched teeth. I looked over my shoulder, back at Nanny, who hunched over the steering wheel.

Did she even know I was gone? She was concentrating awful hard. This was gonna be a long dri—

"Come lie down next to me," Steve said. He sat up, supporting himself with his elbows. Thelma snuggled closer to him.

My stomach dropped. I felt it try to push past my knees and squeeze into my calves. "I can't do that. And why are you here? Thelma, get off that bed."

Thelma only moved her eyeballs to look at me, wrinkling her forehead. She let out a huge sigh.

"I said, get off that bed." I don't think she took me serious, because I was whispering.

"Where are we going?" Steve lay back down. He was so blond and so cute and so tan. I took a step forward then caught myself. It was like, for that one instant, he had hypnotized me.

Demon!

Beguiler!

"How did you get in here? I mean, why? I mean, Nanny is going to have an infarction. I mean, oh no. Thelma."

Thelma slunk off the bed, looking at me like *I* had done something wrong.

"This is not good."

I turned on my heel, took one step forward, slid the curtain in place and walked in slow motion back up to my grandmother, who was going to die, just die, when she found out we had stolen the Simmonses' motor home *and* their kid.

64
No Rest for the Guilty

We'd been on the road for two hours already and were this side of Jacksonville. Turning back now would put us behind four plus hours. I couldn't say anything.

No, I could not say nothing.

So I didn't. I sat in my seat, Nanny driving steady, biting at her lip (maybe she needed a cigarette?). I knew for sure I did and I don't even smoke.

Nanny would find out soon enough. And then what? Why, this would be worse for her health than being microwaved. She was forty-nine after all.

There was no way I would be the one to tell her.

65
Revelation

"What in the hell? What in the hell?"

Nanny braked, not too hard considering we were in something as big as a one-hundred-car train, and flipped on the blinker. I saw her checking out the huge side mirrors. I had to look away. This could prove dangerous. Whether or not we stopped.

"Winston?"

Nanny continued to slow the motor home. "Winston?"

I stared out the side window, watching Florida come to a halt.

"Hey, Miss Jimmie," Stephen said. "Churchill." He gave us both a nod.

I didn't say a thing.

66

No One's Getting Saved

"We gotta talk," Nanny said. "Outside. Winston, you are in big trouble. Get Denny and Thelma." Nanny made three swipes at her cigarettes before she got ahold of them. She had to be thinking kidnapping, like I was.

Thievery and kidnapping. Maybe even grand larceny. Who knew? I bet these offenses would add up to some years in the state penitentiary.

I released Denny from his cage and scooped him up in my arms. "Let's go, Thelma." I kept my voice low. I know Nanny. In the state she was in, well, this part of the highway might explode into flames. She was burning mad.

And I knew, I *knew* without even looking, she blamed me.

67

A Deep, Deep Lie

"Watch out for ants," Steve said. "They're everywhere." He swiped at his leg then hopped a few feet into a safer zone. Thelma jogged up beside him, and the two of them moved out of the weeds where Nanny had parked, to another area, farther from the highway and the red ants and my grandmother.

Nanny walked and struck match after match. Her hands shook. Bad. She almost could have quit smoking by the time she got her cigarette lit. She drew long on it, then marched over to Steve, smoke leaking from her nose. I woulda been scared to death, but he smiled, flicked his long bangs to the side, and waited. He was so cute! And brave. Or maybe, maybe he was dumb. He *should* be terrified of Jimmie Lee Fletcher.

But Steve kept smiling that pretty smile. Thelma sat right there at his side. That dog better not adopt him.

I wanted to adopt him.

Stop that kinda thinking.

"Now, Miss Jimmie, I want you to ponder something."

"Stephen Lovett Simmons." Nanny pointed with her cigarette. She turned to me. "Did you know about this?"

She waved a hand at him, like maybe she could make him disappear.

What?

I pressed my hands against my unbridled chest. "Nanny, are you kidding? How could I know—you came and got *me* this morning and I"—I swallowed—"and I got into the . . . the"—I wouldn't say "stolen"—"vehicle and then *you* drove *me* to here." I pointed to the spot where I stood. A breeze blew in from the ocean that looked as blue as crushed velvet. "How could I know?"

Steve came up next to me, Thelma stuck to his leg. "Oh, Churchill knew, Miss Jimmie," Steve said. "In fact, we were thinking of running away together ourselves in my dear parents' motor home, but you beat us to it. A shotgun wedding in Las Vegas."

"We were not," I said to him. Then I looked at Nanny. "We were not." My voice didn't have much energy. How did he know we were headed to Las Vegas? The boy was a demon.

My grandmother was a thief, and the boy I loved was a demon liar. And my dog? My dog was a traitor. If we hadn't been sixty plus miles from home, I woulda walked on back to the house, crawled into bed, and prayed for a hurricane.

68
Playing

Nanny wouldn't even look at me.

Her cigarette smoldered. So did she.

I came up on her, stepping on tiptoe to avoid her wrath and red ants. "Think about it," I said. I kept my voice smooth as glass. "Logic tells you. How could I know?"

Nanny didn't say anything. Boy, was she cross. If she'd had a flyswatter or a paint stirrer, she might have threatened me. Like when I was a kid.

Sheesh. Nanny's not speaking made me *feel* like I was a little kid.

Fine. I could play this game too. I stomped back to the stolen merchandise and climbed into the front seat.

69
Too Many Feelings

I spent five minutes trying to pick beggar-lice off my socks and shoelaces. I collected them in a little pile to throw away when it wouldn't look like I was rolling down the window so I could hear what my grandmother and the stowaway/kidnap victim were talking about.

Behind them, the ocean crashed. There were some awful nice buildings going up along this stretch of the road. I bet it wouldn't be long before no one could see the ocean at all.

Sigh.

I closed my eyes.

Get past the breakers and I could swim the breast stroke. Great training, an ocean practice. Made pool swimming a breeze.

What was Mark Spitz doing now? They were all in Germany, I knew that. Maybe *he* was swimming in an ocean there. Not that there *was* an ocean there. But there was the English Channel. Sort of.

Could I get good enough to swim the English Channel? Could I try when I was sixteen? Shane Gould was just a little older than me, and she was breaking world records. That gave me—

There was a tap on the window.

"I gotta calm down some," Nanny said, when I lowered the glass. "Smoke another cigarette. You let the dog in. The rooster needs a bit more time out here."

She opened the door, and Thelma jumped in and came up near my feet. I picked at the beggar-lice in her hair. The noon sun burned at us all. Only a few miles of driving comfort, and I was already convinced air-conditioning was a necessity.

Was jail air-conditioned?

Steve clomped into the motor home and sat at the table. I glanced back at him. He watched me through squinty blue eyes. Geez. He could be a model for Sears or in a toothpaste commercial or something.

"I like your dog," he said after a moment. Just like that. Like he wasn't a stowaway. My face warmed up with pleasure. "My mother has one the size of a rat."

I didn't say anything. I knew what dog Steve was talking about. Everyone who went a half mile of Leon's knew. Janet Green Simmons carried the bit of a dog around like a loaf of bread or one big shoe. Ugly little thing, that dog was.

I pulled the last of the beggar-lice from Thelma's belly, and she slipped over to Steve.

"She likes you," I said, catching my breath at this betrayal, "even if you are a stupid ass."

My whole body blushed pink as a setting-sun sky. Now I

was a sinner—a motor-home-car-thief-kidnapping-swearing sinner. Who'd been swimming half nekkid in front of the boy of her dreams, Harlequin-romance style.

Steve raised his eyebrows. "I'm a stupid ass because I wanted to come with you all?"

"You *made* us kidnappers." I whispered the words between the seats, like that might not make them as real.

He shook his head, and Steve's blond hair slipped into his eyes. "Naw," he said. He thumbed his chest. "I am your excuse. You needed a ride. I offered one."

Huh?

I stared at Steve Simmons.

Wait a minute.

Wait. A. Minute. He was right.

"Close your mouth," he whispered, "or I am coming in for another kiss. You are tempting me."

"Gross," I said, then snapped my mouth shut and turned around and faced the long stretch of road in front of us.

70
Feeling A-Okay

The second worst thing? Once I got over my shock? The fact that Stephen had tagged along at all. We started back on I-95, Nanny hitting every pothole next to the highway till she got us on the road.

The worst thing?

I was glad he'd come.

When I was sure Nanny wasn't looking at me, I let myself smile.

71
The Hows and Whys

"He saw me," Nanny said. "Sneaking around a few days ago."

I didn't answer. Just watched Florida pass my window.

"Said he figured I was up to something the way I checked out the rig. Started it. Drove it up and down the driveway."

I raised my eyebrows. *Those* were the only clues?

"Packed up some stuff and waited. Then snuck aboard before I even made my mind up. This morning." Nanny stared out at the road. "Early."

"Well, well, well," I said. Because, sometimes *that's* the best answer to that kind of apology.

72
Privates

We drove until we reached Jacksonville.

"We need to find a place to park," Nanny said. "A place to sleep over." I could see she was nervous as she drove into the traffic of the huge city.

"Look it, Nanny," I said as we passed the sign saying we were welcome to be here, "this is where you were born."

"I know that, Winston," Nanny said.

She was back to normal. As normal as she could be anyway. I could tell by her voice. Maybe she had settled herself down to the fact we were felons. Big time felons.

Nanny stopped at the Sinclair dinosaur station to get fuel.

The attendant got the gas pumping for us, then headed to clean the windows.

"I'm using the potty," Nanny said.

"We got one in here," I said. "It's small, but nice." Sheesh. I sounded like an advertisement.

Nanny slid out the door. "I wanna relieve myself where I'm still when I sit down. Let Denny out for a minute."

"Geez, Nanny," I said. My face turned bright red. I could feel the heat, like an inside-out sunburn.

Steve watched Nanny leave the motor home. "It's no big deal," he said. "We all pee and . . ."

"Thanks," I said, and watched the attendant scrub at the love-bugs squished on the front windshield.

73
Sidetracked for a Moment

Nanny came out from the side of the gas station waving a handful of paper.

"What in the world?"

Denny and I stood—well, I stood and he hopped—on the grass where the green Sinclair dinosaur looked off toward the west.

"Are you thinking of my momma?" I asked the dinosaur, turning from my grandmother, who seemed like she was the youngest grandmother anyone knew, the way she trotted out the bathroom waving colored papers over her head.

I petted the dinosaur's neck as Denny hopped around, pecking at this and that. "My momma is off in Las Vegas. She asked us to come get her." Both stayed mute, and I felt like I was four all over again, watching Momma drive away and leave me with Nanny and a stuffed teddy bear.

A truck loaded with guys drove past and beeped. One yelled out, "Great chicken, baby!"

Good grief. How could a typical boy not know the difference between a rooster and a chicken? A hot wind tugged at my hair, highway air all around me like a mini tornado, smelling of asphalt and fuel.

"Come see this, Winston," Nanny said. She worked her way across the concrete. For a moment the motor home kept me from seeing her, and I had a flash, an almost-not-there flash, of life without her. My heart tried to get free of my body.

"A map," Nanny hollered, her voice scooting under a couple of cars and our own stolen vehicle. "Show's the hospital where I was born. And things to do here in Jacksonville."

She was here still. Here and loud as ever.

"Let's get going back to Nanny, Denny," I said, and scooped him up close to my heart, where he looked at me first with one eye and then the other.

74
Setting Things Straight

"You know," Nanny said, settling a seat belt across her lap, "the oldest American pachyderm zoo is right here in this city and it's early yet."

Thelma looked at Nanny from where her head rested in Steve's lap. He sat on the built-in sofa, arms stretched out like he was ready to hug the world. Or me. He could hug me. The way Thelma lay there, so relaxed and full of betrayal, I was surprised that Denny hadn't roosted on Steve's shoulder.

"Yup, right here in Jacksonville," Nanny said.

"Take's a while to fill this tank," I said, 'cause what else can you say when your grandmother is talking about pachyderms when she should be returning a stolen boy and vehicle and ignoring my ne'er-do-well mother?

"What?" Steve said. He leaned forward. "What do you mean?"

"Elephants." Nanny and I said the word together.

"Oh." He nodded and sat back on the sofa.

Nanny flapped the pamphlets under my nose. "And there's a great big ol' tree. In a park. Protected by the government."

I didn't answer.

"I love elephants," she whispered. She tapped at her lips like she held a cigarette between her fingers.

"Nanny," I said. "I hate to pop your bubble, but we don't have time. If we're gonna visit around I suggest we go on back home. Maybe make a plan of selling our place and your part of the business and then make a few more plans for moving on accounta all the consequences we are gonna have to face."

"What makes you think we are getting caught, Winston?" Nanny stared at me like I'd lost my mind.

I blinked. Had I?

The pressure was getting to me—boys, grandmothers, elephants. And we weren't even out of Florida yet.

I swallowed. "If you want to go get Momma, we gotta get."

"You're right, Winston," Nanny said. "You. Are. Right. Truth is, we don't have time for potty breaks or cigarette stops. We have to drive like a bat outta heck."

In his cage, Denny ruffled his feathers. Bats make him nervous, I think. Or almost-swearing.

"We don't have time for sleep." Nanny set the pamphlets (advertising a huge oak tree and elephants, I now saw) on the floor between us.

Three cars came and went while we filled the motor home. I was hungry. And nervous. I wanted to turn and stare at Steve. I felt the need look at his all-over cuteness. Or else call Thelma over to snuggle on my lap. Not that she wanted to spend any time with me now. I think she had a crush on Steve too.

"Wish I could take us straight through. Wish we didn't have to stop at all. Not even for a free chance to view the elephants," Nanny said.

And then from that sofa came, "I can drive."

75

Payday

The gas station attendant tapped on Nanny's window, and she paid him, gasping at the cost.

"Thirty-six cents a gallon, ma'am," he said. "And this here is a big rig." He patted the side of the motor home like he loved it. "Great way to travel."

For a moment I wondered if Mike (so said his name tag) would invite himself along on our trip. But Nanny didn't give him a chance. She smiled, took her forty-two cents change, and pulled out of the station, hitting only one part of the concrete divider with the back wheels.

"Careful, miss," Mike yelled after us.

And we were back on the road again.

76

Driving?

Nanny didn't waste any time lecturing.

"Stephen Lovett Simmons. I know as well as the next person in line that you aren't anywhere near sixteen yet. Don't you got like six months?"

He shrugged when I glanced over at him. "I been driving for a long time." He said this like he and I were the only ones in the motor home. "Plus I got my learner's permit. Have had it for a while."

Nanny sent me a squirrely look. I've been driving forever too. I *don't* have a permit. Yet.

"I'm best at night driving," Steve said. "I've had more practice."

He stood and stretched, pressing his hands flat on the ceiling.

I faced the front, fast. He needed to buy longer shirts. Or pull his shorts up.

"Not-even-sixteen-year-olds can't drive at night," Nanny said. She reached for her pack of cigarettes, whose green packaging reflected in the windshield, and then held them in her lap. "It's against the law."

I never drive at night.

"Since we're being honest"—I had to do a double take when Steve said that—"I drive when I'm *borrowing* Dad's car. After everyone's in bed. You know." He said this all matter-of-fact.

No, I didn't know. What did this mean? He stole from his father? His car? I mean, sure, it's bad to steal from your employer/co-owner, but your very own dad?

"Hrmph," Nanny said.

Trying my luck, I checked out Steve again. He gave me a slow wink. How could a wink be so slow? And so cute.

My mouth smiled without my meaning for it to.

"Me and Churchill here—" Steve said, getting up and standing behind our seats, where I could feel the heat from his body. Or was that the afternoon sun beating in on me? "—can drive once the sun sets. You can sleep in the back, Miss Jimmie. We'll make good time that way. Drive straight through stopping only to fill this beast and get food and stuff. You both already bought some things so we should be good for a while. You know, not needing to stop and all that."

Nanny's silence seemed to suggest she might be considering Steve's offer.

"I don't think I can drive when it's dark," I said. My voice was a whisper. Thelma pushed her head up next to Steve's leg and he petted her.

"I can teach you," he said, and looked me right in the eye.

77

Worries

Nanny had me make dinner. Then she made me feed her the peanut butter and jelly sandwich. I wasn't sure why. I'd seen her cook lobster, steam broccoli, and run out for a smoke all in less than ten minutes and using just one hand. Could this motor home be causing her this much grief? Perhaps guilt had something to do with her nerves.

"You worried?" I asked her as I helped her sip Coke from the bottle.

"What?"

Denny sat on my seat while I knelt beside Nanny.

Steve had a guitar (where had *that* come from?) and was tuning it.

"I said are you worried?"

Nanny sort of looked at me, not quite taking her eyes off the road. We were headed to Tallahassee now and the traffic was thick. Maybe people were going to New Smyrna to help find a lost teen. "Not really."

"Seems it."

Steve strummed the guitar and in a moment started singing. Dang it! He sang the dumbest song this year, "A Horse with No Name." He sounded pretty darn good. His peanut butter and jelly sandwich balanced on his knee. And look at that. Thelma didn't even try to lick it. Had that been my dinner she would have swallowed it whole.

What was this? It seemed all of nature conspired against me.

"I started headed west in a rig with no name," Steve sang. "It felt good to be out of my home. Headed west, you can remember your name . . ."

"I mean," I said, trying my best to ignore Steve, "you're gripping the steering wheel. And you have to look a hundred years older the way you're driving."

"What?" Nanny swerved a little and someone behind us beeped. Out the window Florida seemed to not have an ocean nearby. "That was rude."

"You got a bug up your butt and it's noticeable to other drivers."

Nanny took a swig of Coke, her lips coming out like a camel's toward the bottle I held. Then she let out a long sigh.

"It's your momma," she said. "I'm concerned for your momma."

I flopped down on the floor so I didn't wear my legs out before I had a chance to swim. Whenever that would be.

"There's nothing new about those worries."

That's the whole truth. Nanny still worries over my momma all these years later, even when we never hear from her months at a time. Even when she hasn't seen her in a decade.

Momma. My eyes went all squinchy and I couldn't even stop it. She wasn't a momma at all. Not a daughter. She was a somebody me and Nanny didn't know anymore.

And why Nanny felt such concern was beyond me. But I kept my mouth shut.

Again Nanny sighed. "You're right, Winston, yes you are. I got to keep positive. Smile. Not be so uptight. I got me a case of the nerves right when we pulled out of New Smyrna and headed north."

"That was fear, Nanny. Fear because the police and FBI are gonna be after you."

Nanny puckered her lips again so I could give her another sip. "That's all for now," she said after swallowing. "I'm gonna trust you on this one, Winston. Sometimes a girl has to do what a girl has to do. And I have to do this."

I set the Coke bottle down with a thunk. Thelma looked at me.

"Nanny," I said, and put my arms around her neck. I kissed her face. "Loosen up and enjoy the trip. We got us some real driving to do. You wanna be sick the whole way? Momma needs help and you aim to do that."

"Winston," Nanny said. Her voice was all soft and mushy. She gave me a quick look then stared back at the road. "You are the best girl a grandmother could have."

78

Singing

"A Horse with No Name," with new words, went on way too long. All of about five minutes. Then I'd had enough. Want to ruin my disposition? Play music I can't stand. Like something from the band America.

At last I slid on the sofa near Steve. "You know 'Bobby McGee'?" I said.

He gave a little nod, changed his fingering, and started playing.

"Don't mess with the words this time," I said. I scooted closer still and our knees touched. It felt like someone had struck a match on my kneecap.

"That's gotta be my favorite song ever," Nanny said. "I am so sorry that Janet Joplin is gone."

"Janis, Nanny," I said.

Steve smiled, dipped his head a bit over the guitar. Looked at me all squinty eyed. "I love your grandmother," he said. And then: "You sing?"

"Maybe," I said. "A little."

The truth is, all the Fletchers, from start to finish, can sing. Nanny herself sang with her sisters on the radio when they were teens. I know it! Who knew there was a radio way back when?

"Are you joking, Steve?" Nanny said. She said this kinda slow and her hands looked all clenchy. "Winston can sing any part out there. Anything but bass. We sing in the choir at our church. If I could coax her, I'd have the girl singing in school choir. And maybe on television."

I shot a glance at the back of Nanny's head. "I'd rather swim," I said.

Steve gazed at me. Like right-in-the-eye gazing. "I know she's a good swimmer," he said. "I saw that my own self." He moved his mouth close to my ear. "Looked sexy. Yes, you did."

I felt my face grow warm. Who said that boy should be able to control my embarrassment genes? And how much had he seen? I had done the back stroke, nekkid.

"You know she's hoping to be an Olympian?"

"Nanny," I said. "Shhh. Don't say anything about anything."

"I *didn't* know," Steve said. He kept strumming the guitar. Doing this little almost smile. And burning me with his matchlike knee.

"No one does," I said. "I keep private things private." I said the last part loud so Nanny would get the hint. She didn't.

"She wants to be a Mark Spitz." Nanny let out a laugh of genuine pride. "A *female* Mark Spitz."

Steve raised his eyebrows. "A Shane Gould," he said.

My tone was reverent. "Yes," I said.

"Too sexy for that," he whispered, looking through his bangs at me.

What would Angel do right now? Laugh and pretend to hit Steve? Show him her tan lines? Smack her grandmother? "Let's sing," I said.

The music put me in mind of how Janis Joplin had overdosed and died when she should still be singing and how Nanny wouldn't let me play too much Alice Cooper when she was in the house and how Roger Miller was played down at Leon's restaurant 'cause he stops in for a meal on occasion. Music can do that to you. Take you anywhere.

It can ease the thought the boy you loved had seen you in your birthday suit. Well, a birthday suit that included undies.

We sang halfway to Mobile, Alabama, then Nanny said, "Go rest, Stephen Lovett. I'm turning the driving over to you soon as the sun goes down."

79

Sleeping Arrangements

Steve set the guitar down and stood. He rocked with the movement of the motor home.

Outside the sky took on that late afternoon look. Sort of tired and damp and ready-for-evening that the South gets after a day of too-hot-for-comfort.

"You better rest, too, Winston," Nanny said. "I can't have him driving alone. I'll get us out of Mobile, then wake you both."

"Okay," I said.

I climbed over Denny and went to where the bag of my things sat. My pillow was on top.

"I'll crash here, if you want me to," Steve said, and gestured at the sofa. "It pulls out into a bed, you know."

Would wonders never cease? "Are you kidding?" I said.

Steve shook his head. "No. I mean it." He grinned at me, like I was a little kid or something.

For some reason I felt like my own feathers had gotten ruffled. Every joint in my body stiffened. "Some people don't have money to throw away," I said, under my breath. "Some people don't have money for fancy stuff."

"What?" Steve said, and he made to grab my hand, but I moved out of his reach.

"Go sleep in the bed at the back," I said. Tears stung my eyes. Sheesh, I *was* tired! My feelings were hurt. How could that be?

"What did I do?" Steve said. "Did I say something wrong?"

I shook my head. The tears cooled my eyeballs off.

"Feeling sensitive?" Steve said. He ducked his face close to mine.

"Get a move on, you two," Nanny said. "We got miles to go before we sleep."

Steve walked the couple of steps until he stood in front of the stove. I clutched the pillow to my chest.

Cute. He was so cute! My feathers settled right down. He stepped back to me again.

"You should come sleep by me," he said, whispering. "In the back. It's more comfortable than the sofa bed or the one above the cabin." He slid a bit closer. I could have let him kiss me, but Steve didn't try.

"Are you kidding? Nanny would rather run over us both with this bus of a vehicle before she allowed that."

A picture of Angel popped into my head. Had they . . . ? Had they . . . ? You know. Done. It. You know. Together.

Steve stepped past me. "All I'm saying, Churchill, is it's kinda nice to be swayed to sleep." He grinned then touched my arm. His hand was so warm my stomach skipped a beat. No wait. My heart skipped a beat and my stomach lurched like we had hit a pothole big as Ohio.

80
Visitor

Steve was right. Sleeping in the motor home was comfortable. Not a thing like lying down in the back seat of our old Dodge.

I was out for what seemed only a moment.

When I woke, the sky was dark as pitch, and both Denny and Thelma sat in the front seat, in my place.

Nanny smoked and drove with her knees on the steering wheel. There was ash on the floor, and I was too tired, almost, to hold my eyes open.

"You can't smoke in here," I said. "We gotta keep this place looking and smelling clean as a whistle. Otherwise the Simmonses are gonna know we stole from them."

But Nanny didn't answer.

The curtains opened in the back, and Mark Spitz, wet and wearing a Speedo, came to where I sat. His mustache dripped water.

"What are you doing here?" I said. "Did you win a medal?"

I could smell the pool. Mark Spitz flicked water on my face, and I jerked awake trying to remember where I was, my heart pounding.

"Nanny?"

She didn't answer, maybe because my voice was a whisper.

"Thelma?"

Where was I? Nanny ran off the road a bit and I remembered everything. Our lawlessness, my mother, Steve.

I glanced her way. She still sat hunched over the steering wheel, but no cigarette burned. Thelma was no place to be seen, though it was hard to see anything toward the back of the rig it was so dark.

"Go to sleep, Winston," Nanny said. "You got another couple of hours to rest."

How did she know I was awake?

Somehow she always knows.

"'Kay." I turned over and was soothed to sleep.

81

A Break in the Trip

The next time I woke, it was for real, to Nanny pulling over. We bounced every which way.

When we came to a halt, a real halt (not a slow creeping up on a halt), there was the smell of salt water and I could hear the crash of waves.

I sat up, feeling dizzy. Steve pushed through the curtains, Thelma trailing behind. They looked like ghosts—a good-looking boy ghost and a used-to-be-the-best-dog-in-the-world ghost.

"So you met someone . . . Goody, goody," popped into my head, and in my mind I saw Shelley Winters wielding a knife from the movie *What's the Matter with Helen?* Nanny was right. I needed to stop going to the movie house to watch thrillers.

Now Nanny swiveled around in her chair. Light from outside made her face eerie too. What was this? An Alfred Hitchcock film? "Thought we could take a break, stretch our legs . . ."

"Get a smoke," I said.

" . . . and walk the beach," Nanny said, glaring at me, "before we get on our way again. Some time here on the Gulf will be good."

Thelma stretched out long, her tail pointing to the motor home roof. She sort of glanced in my direction and gave me a nod. Then she padded over so I could pet her head.

"I love that dog of yours," Steve said.

Twice now, he loved something from my family. I swallowed. Thelma eased back by his side.

"She's a man's dog. A real dog."

"You mean a *girl's* dog, raised and trained by girls," I said, but Steve didn't seem to hear.

"A dog you can hunt with. Not a dog the size of your shoe. Yes sirree, I love this dog." He squatted to pet her. She laid her head on his chest, right under his chin.

"Me too," I said. "I love her too." My mouth tasted like a dirty sock—and felt as dry. I scrunched my eyebrows, disappointment in Thelma traveling in my vital organs.

But, sheesh, could I blame her? Steve looked TV ready, his hair kinda messy, his teeth so white. How did he do that, first thing? I bet he didn't even have stinky breath. Maybe the sweet smell of chocolate milk. For sure, I needed to go brush.

I made my way to the bathroom, used the facilities, then scrubbed at my teeth. It was time for a clothes change, too, so I slipped on different shorts and an old button-up that was a coupla sizes too big.

Outside the vehicle, I could hear banging and feel a thumping come from under my feet.

Where were we? Did they have earthquakes here?

I hurried out into the evening.

No one. Not even Denny.

They'd left without me.

Forgotten me?

The moon, shining light thick as sweet cream, splashed down.

Everything was quiet. So quiet. Except for the ocean, which I couldn't see—it had to be on the other side of the Simmonses' motor home. No other sounds. What time was it?

I reached toward the moon, going up on my tiptoes, then breathed deep and caught a whiff of Nanny's cigarette. I walked toward the sound of the waves, where I was sure I'd find my family and the jailbait.

What I didn't expect was the ocean to look like a movie ocean, made of dark blue and almost-white colors.

The group of them moved toward the shoreline, Denny hopping along on his leash, Thelma running ahead with Steve, who carried a surfboard (what?), Nanny's cigarette glowing when she turned to me and called out, "Come on, Winston. We don't got all night."

82

The Gulf

The Gulf looked like a cake with shiny icing. Waves rolled in, but they weren't huge. The water was calm enough to do some decent swimming in. This place was way more tranquil than New Smyrna Beach.

I turned and ran back into the motor home.

My bag. My bathing suit. A towel.

In moments I was changed, leaving all my clothes on the tiny bathroom floor. Then I ran out the door again, leaping to the parking lot pavement.

Mark Spitz, I thought. I could almost see him from my dream. Mark Spitz and the 1976 Olympics for me, if I wasn't doing time because of our unwise decision-making in moments of severe stress.

By now, Nanny walked the shoreline, giving Denny plenty of time to hop this way and that. Steve was in the water. These nighttime waves in the Gulf of Mexico weren't the same as what we got over on the East Coast.

"Winston," Nanny said as I ran past her, "you be careful."

Olympics. Here I come.

The water was warm and in a moment I was diving through a wave, swimming hard against the current, and popping up in time to ride a gentle swell up and down.

This was the life.

83

Gulf Swimming

I swam till Nanny called me closer and my arms were tired.

"You two," she said when Steve and me stood knee-deep in the waves. Water ran down my face, down my back, dripped off my fingertips. "This sound is putting me to sleep. Fifteen more minutes for the both of you, then you get back in and we leave. I'm going in to bed. Make sure you dry Thelma off good before you bring her in our little home away from home and don't track any sand into that vehicle. We will never get all that out."

"Yes ma'am, Miss Jimmie," Steve said.

"A few more minutes than fifteen," I said. "Please, Nanny."

Nanny walked off like I hadn't spoken, and I knew the answer was no the way she kept walking.

"Dang it," I said.

"Kiss me, Churchill," Steve said.

Sure thing, I thought, but I said nothing. Did snot run down my face? I swallowed. Why did I walk toward him? I should wait until I knew Nanny wouldn't look back and see us. I needed to take this time to swim, while I could. I only had fifteen minutes.

Fifteen minutes.

Enough time, Patty Bailey said, to have sex. I pushed Patty Bailey's voice away.

My body walked toward Steve, who held on to his surfboard with one arm and reached toward me with the other. My mind worked. Mark Spitz. Olympics. A thousand miles to drive.

"Gotta swim while I can," I said, as Steve's hand closed around nothing but air.

I dove into the water to practice in the moonlit night in my last few minutes of freedom.

84
Copilot

The highway was deserted, only a few cars traveling against us, only a few that passed. The cypress grew up like giants out of the water to our right. When I squinted, staring at the trees, they seemed to change to slender ladies, with moss for hair, arms dipping or reaching for the heavens, all of them standing in tar.

I worked my way down the hall, pulled the shade down in the kitchen, and went to the front of the motor home. Nanny had climbed up on the bed above us. I knew why. To keep an eye and ear out to whatever me and Steve thought to do while we drove. How embarrassing.

"Churchill," Steve said when I sat in the passenger seat. He sounded pleased. "You're back."

We'd been driving down the highway for a while now. The swim, the warm water, had made me sleepy. I'd washed the Gulf and salt away. Thought, while I stood in the tiny shower, how a boy was driving toward Vegas. The cutest boy in all of New Smyrna Beach, Florida. I'd bit my lip.

Now my hair was still bound up by a towel.

"I'm back." I pulled the towel loose and let my damp

hair go. It sprung into corkscrew curls. In the moonlight it looked the color of good silverware.

Was I going to be able to stay awake long enough to help drive?

Swimming is the best thing to put you to sleep. And ocean swimming wears you out.

"You're good at that water thing." Steve drove with both hands, but he did his driving like he did his surfing. So natural it looked like maybe he was born to take this trip with us. "I can see you in the Olympics."

I grinned. "Really? I sure hope so. I got things to do with my life." I stepped over Thelma and settled myself in the seat.

Steve sort of looked at me. A passing car lit his face, and when he smiled, my heart did that Grinch thing and grew a little bigger. "Swimming things?"

I nodded. "Swimming things," I said.

"Nothing else?"

"Like what?" I said. I pulled at my hair, trying to comb through it with my fingers. I needed my pick. "Do you mean like college?"

He shrugged. "Sure. Or business."

I pulled my feet into the seat. "You think I want to always bus tables at your daddy's restaurant? The answer is no. Maybe start a different restaurant for me and Nanny ourselves. Maybe."

Steve looked at me a long second.

"Watch the road," I said.

"I can see it."

"No you can't. You're looking at me."

"I can drive with my eyes shut," he said.

"Well, don't."

He stared at the road a minute then closed his eyes.

"What are you doing?" I straightened up in my seat. The towel fell to the floor.

"Showing you my talents."

"Open your eyes!"

"I'm telling you, I can drive with my eyes closed. I have a sixth sense."

"Stephen."

"I like it when you say my name that way."

The motor home never left the road, but stayed right between the white and yellow lines. He was pretty darn good at driving blind, but . . . "Open your eyes!" My voice was something of a whispered screech. "Nanny is gonna skin us both alive."

Instead, Steve turned and glanced at me. His right eye was closed. The left, open.

"You jerk," I said. Then laughed.

85
Almost Night Driving

We drove with the late-night radio playing. Out of Orange, Texas. Into Beaumont, Texas. Another state down. Whew.

Jackson Browne, Cher, Dr. Hook. Donny Osmond, Carly Simon, Neil Diamond. Roberta Flack, the Jackson 5, and even a bit of *Jesus Christ Superstar*.

The sky was covered with clouds now. Lightning was blinding, even at this distance.

"Probably a twister coming," Steve said.

"Probably," I said. I slept sitting up. I fought to stay awake, but my body wasn't having any of that. As I slipped off to sleep, Thelma came up to sit next to Steve and keep him company while he drove.

Then someone said, "Winston Churchill. You are something else."

"What?" I said. My eyes snapped open. Electricity sliced the sky in half. Pecan pie sounded great.

"You're dreaming," Thelma said.

"Yes, I am," I said.

86
Sleeping on the Road

I woke up on the sofa, Nanny pulling into a Phillips gas station.

"Guess where we're headed?" she said.

I blinked. Cleared my throat.

"That's right. San Antonio. You know what's there?"

I tried to speak.

"The Alamo."

"Oh." There it was. My voice back.

"You know what happened at that historic site?"

I opened my mouth.

"Your great-great-uncle twice removed fought against the Mexicans and was shot in the neck."

"Huh? I didn't know," I said. "You never told me that story."

"I forgot about this particular relative." Nanny nodded once like the nod might cement the telling in her brain.

"How far have we gone?"

"Since Houston—which you slept through—almost two hundred miles. I got lost only once. Stevie helped me get on track. Thank goodness Leon Simmons is armed with a road atlas." Nanny gestured at the book of maps on the dashboard.

"Who's Stevie?" I sat up. Yes sirree, I could get used to sleeping in a moving vehicle. Seeing there was a refrigerator less than three feet from my sleeping spot. And a place to potty. This was the life. Not including the illegal stuff, but I could put that all out of my head. I went to look through the fridge for something to eat. I came back with a big container of yogurt and an apple.

"I wonder how the hens are," Nanny said. "How Doris is doing as front-end manger. Think the restaurant is doing okay without me?"

"No, ma'am," I said. I opened the yogurt. "Business has slowed since we left. But don't you worry. It'll pick up once you get back to arm wrestle it into shape." I bit into the apple and wished, right away, that I had chosen an orange instead.

"Smart alecks never prosper," Nanny said.

"Are you sure?" I flopped onto the sofa.

Outside, storm clouds swirled. The Texas sky looked like a Florida sky right before the heavens open and angels dump truckloads of water on us. The attendant washed down the windows. Didn't he see it was gonna rain? It sure was taking a long time for the tank to fill. Again. I let out a morning sigh, fanning at my gross morning yogurt breath.

"Wish you'd put that in a bowl," Nanny said. "One of these days I am sending a request to yogurt companies around the world asking them to make individual containers of yogurt so you—" She pointed at me. There was an unlit cigarette between her fingers. "—stop contaminating breakfast."

"I know," I said.

Nanny paid for gas after the tank was full and started out of the station just as the rain fell. The drops were light, sometimes disappearing before they hit the ground, then falling heavier.

"Where's Steve?"

"Sleeping."

I moved to the front of the motor home.

"Nanny," I said, after I had crunched the last of the meat off the apple, "tell me about you and Steve's daddy."

87
The Telling

Nanny looked at me side eyed. She puffed at the unlit cigarette. "Making this last," she said, saluting me with it.

"I mean, I know you loved him. That he was your only true love . . ."

"I loved your grandfather, God rest his soul."

Nanny says that anytime she mentions Mike, who ran off right after Nanny got pregnant. Kinda like my momma, except Momma was six months till seventeen when I was born. Nanny was seventeen her own self, when she got my momma as her baby. As you can see, this is a pattern. A pattern I plan to break. Maybe I will never have babies, but for sure I will do it with a husband. Or when I am super old, like twenty-five.

"I am sure you loved him," I said.

The rain came down harder.

"We're headed straight into the storm," Nanny said. "I hope to goodness we drive through this baby so I can see the Alamo."

"Tell me the truth," I said.

Like God was involved, a sign came up on the side of the road. We had a good ways to go till the Alamo (hey, a rhyme!) and with Steve asleep, this was a perfect chance for Nanny to spill her guts. "We got forty-eight miles more till you can see where your cousin twice removed got shot in the neck."

Nanny let out a long sigh. She looked at me then sighed again.

"You know sighing isn't allowed in the Fletcher home," I said. "You been sighing a lot."

Nanny ignored me. "Put on your seat belt," she said. She took a drag on her cigarette. Then she started talking.

88
Texas Rain

"Leon and I went to school together."

I nodded. Rolled down the window and threw the apple core onto the side of the road, watching it bounce away. Rain splattered in on my arm. "I know that part. I know about you loving each other and all that. How he broke your heart. I guess I want to know how Steve's mom got into the act."

"Let me tell the story the way I want to."

"Fine."

"You know we dated right up until your grandfather came into my life." Nanny tsked. "Now he was a looker."

"And a runner," I said. Lightning split the sky wide open. I shivered.

"Tornado weather," Nanny said. "So, as you know, your granddaddy and I got pregnant and he took off and—"

"Why didn't you go back to Leon?"

"Here." Nanny handed me her cigarette. "Put this away."

I slid the cigarette, with red lipstick on the filter, into the Winston Salem package.

"He didn't want me then and I didn't blame him. In fact, I didn't even try to get back with him."

No.

"What?"

"I was pregnant with your momma, Judith Lee. His momma, Miss Dorothy, never approved of me. She died—from meanness, I think—and me and Leon started the restaurant. You know, a few years later. But we never dated again."

It was hard to see out the window. The sky was the color of an avocado.

"I've loved him from afar ever since. I'd never tell him of course, but that's the God's honest truth." Nanny glanced at me, quick, then at the road.

"That is the saddest story I ever did hear," I said. I'd eaten a good fourth of the yogurt. Maybe I should save some for later. Or for Steve.

Nanny spoke so low, it was like she was talking to herself. The windshield fogged up and she had me turn on the defroster.

"Sure is," she said. And then, "I gotta find a place to pull over. Look for rest area signs, Winston."

"Yes, ma'am."

We pulled over twenty minutes later.

"He waited years to get married. All that time we worked together and built the business, and then he found Stevie's momma, who happens to be almost half his age."

With the motor home stopped the windows fogged

over some more. I heard Steve get up and get into the shower. Thelma sauntered to the door and whined. When I opened up the place to outside, she stared through the screen at the rain.

"Not interested?" I said.

Thelma slunk away and went to wait outside the bathroom for Steve.

89
What I Didn't Know

Nanny and I sat in silence a long time. Till the water went off. Till Steve walked out of the shower and toward the bedroom, a towel wrapped low around his hips, his hair slick and dripping.

"The worst part . . . ," Nanny said. She spoke as if she had to tell me a secret but didn't look me in the eye. "The worst part was after Steve was born, his momma tried to buy me out of the business and then when I wouldn't go for it, she pitched a fit till Leon all but stopped talking to me. Me and Leon? We haven't worked a full shift together since. I work the front. He manages everything. We only talk business." She paused. "It's like parts of my heart have been sliced out of my chest. A bit when your momma left. A bit more when Leon listened to his wife and stopped giving me the time of day."

The air felt too humid to breathe. "I didn't know this," I said.

Nanny stood and shook herself out. She went to the back, where she pulled out a raincoat.

"Some things a mother figure keeps from her kid," she said.

90

More Storm

Nanny walked Thelma (who stayed out long enough to do her business then hurried in to shake off, splashing everyone) and Denny (who ruffled his feathers a time or two then hopped and pecked at the ground). She stood in the rain, that slanted west now, like it pointed the direction we should go, protecting her cigarette that glowed every time she puffed on it. At long last, Nanny came into the motor home, toweled Denny off, then herself, and gave him a handful of corn on a paper plate. I set to drying off Thelma, picking at black hair that left her body and clung between my fingers.

Nanny was sure there was a tornado going on *somewhere* in Texas. The sky stayed dark with that tint of green. The rained pounded at us, hitting sometimes straight down from the sky, sometimes from the left, and sometimes from the right.

When Steve came out, dressed in surf shorts and an old ratty T-shirt, wearing a pair of flip-flops, the five of us settled to wait out the storm. Wind buffeted the vehicle, and the sky turned even more scary looking.

"As I thought," Nanny said, but it was hard to hear her,

the rain fell so. She picked at her thumbnail. I would say, watching her, that my grandmother was nervous.

Cars passed on the highway going awful slow.

Hail the size of quarters slammed against the motor home, and other cars pulled in next to us to wait things out.

"If we need to . . . ," Nanny said. "If I see a tornado, we run over there."

Nanny pointed to the squat building almost hidden by trees. The rest stop. "Bathrooms are a good place to be in tornadoes."

"There's a good place to be in a tornado?" Steve looked a little nervous too. Good. He wasn't perfect. I stretched. Acted calm.

In the distance we heard sirens, and the radio reported tornado sightings in several towns I didn't recognize and called the weather a freak of nature. I wondered if it stormed in Germany. What was going on there?

"Get the cards, Winston," Nanny said, after I had made myself comfortable. What was she so worried about? Tornado, shornado. I knew in my gut we would be okay.

Plus nothing would stop Nanny from getting her kid. Nothing. I knew that, too, and I bet this weather did and so did God. My grandmother clapped her hands together. "We're gonna ride this little bit of a hindrance out in style, like we do at home."

91
Cards

We played poker until the weather cleared.

Nanny won every hand.

"She cheats, I think," I said to Steve, who was getting his butt handed to him by a front-end restaurant manager. We sat at the little table, chips spilled out in the middle of it. Nanny had herself a few good stacks piled on the table just left of her elbow. Red. Blue. White. Little towers growing ever taller. "She could clean up in Vegas, but she refuses to be a betting woman."

The wind shook the motor home like a big ol' hand had hold of us and was checking to see who all was in here.

"Is that so, Miss Jimmie?"

An unlit cigarette dangled from Nanny's lips. "Devil's play, that's what betting is," she said. "And I am too cheap to lose even a penny."

"Who taught you to play this game?" Steve said.

Nanny paused. Smiled. "Why, your daddy. When we were in eighth grade." Nanny smiled some more. What did she remember right now? What made her smile like that?

Would Steve teach me something? My stomach tumbled over.

"Really?" Steve nodded, like maybe he didn't believe Nanny.

"Why?" I shuffled the cards. They were worn in that perfect way, so they moved together smooth. I made a bridge, then, when I thought the cards were good and mixed, dealt everyone a hand.

"My daddy plays every card game *except* poker."

"Is that right?" I said.

Nanny didn't flinch like I woulda. She didn't rise to the challenge or say, *You calling me a liar?* No, she looked over the cards in her hand, moving things this way and that.

"Hit me," Steve said, shifting cards around.

Did Leon ever talk about Nanny to Steve? I had a strong feeling the two had never spoken of Leon's first love—my grandmother—and the thought was frustrating.

92
Plans

When we pulled out on the road again, Texas looked wetter than a kitchen mop.

Rain still fell, and cars drove through puddles of water that sometimes looked the size of a small lake. They splashed waves big enough to surf on.

Nanny had spent some time giving Steve card-playing tips. Like, "Some people say to have a poker face. I believe in having a 'fool 'em' face. Pretend like you might have something when you don't at all." Or, "Lose every once in a while, makes you appear vulnerable." Or, "Don't be afraid to take your time getting your moves down right."

Steve glanced at me on that one. I practiced a poker stare.

"Never knew none of this," he said. He slipped a rubber band that had almost lost all its stretch around the deck, then handed the cards to me so I could put them in our grocery-bag suitcase. "I'm gonna win me some coin from the guys at school." He looked at me. "You know Aufhammer? Benjy Aufhammer? He's a running back on the team?"

I nodded, though I had never watched one school game and I didn't plan to. (*Not even if Steve is your boyfriend? Or you kiss him again? Or . . .* "Not even," I told myself.)

"He's a shark. Cleans my clock every time we play any card game."

"Shouldn't be betting," Nanny said. She held on to the steering wheel now like it was a life preserver. Every time she headed toward a puddle on the highway she slowed. Once someone even beeped and flipped her off as he passed, sending water splashing at the windshield. "Got better things to do with your time, Steve. Got a business to run one of these days."

Nanny sent Steve, who sat in my place up front, a side-eyed look.

Steve shook his head. "Not interested in food. I mean, no offense, seeing you and my dad been working that place forever. I'd rather surf. Or"—he shrugged—"or play cards for a living. Or build houses. Don't want to stay indoors all the time."

"Nothing wrong with that," Nanny said, but in the rearview, I could see her lips were pinched.

Denny hopped around the dining area, or whatever this part of the motor home was called, on the spread-out newspaper. When he could, he pecked at the shag rug. Then after a moment he went and settled himself near Nanny.

Thelma pretended I wasn't around.

"That's not what my dad says. He wants me to keep the business in the family."

"I can see that," Nanny said, and she gripped the steering wheel all the tighter.

93

The Alamo

We circled the Alamo three times, Nanny making Steve drive.

At one corner, she had him stop, and me and Nanny went out into the pouring rain that was like a slippery gray sheet.

"He coulda been shot right here," Nanny said.

"Who? Steve?"

"No, our relative."

I looked at the sidewalk. "Wasn't he in the fort?" I said.

"In the neck, girl," Nanny said, and I saw she was pointing at her throat.

"I guess so," I said. I took in a damp breath. "What are you contemplating? I see it all over your face. But I need to tell you something, Nanny. I'm not so sure I want the restaurant either. I'm thinking of something of my own. Something new."

Nanny gave me a look. It was long and sort of drippy, seeing how the rain hadn't let up one bit and I was soaked through to my underwear. I clasped my arms tight over my breasts that I knew showed through this shirt.

"We'll do what we gotta do when the time comes," Nanny said, and then she went and patted the fort, all reverent-like and said, "Let's get on in that bus, dry off, and hit the road."

94

More Mark

Coming out of the storm and heading toward the middle of Texas, Nanny turned on the news where we heard the Olympics (including Mark Spitz!) had started.

"I want him to win one medal," I said. "Just one gold medal. I know he's setting his sights on seven wins. But if he gets just one, I'll be happy." I smiled. "No one in the world swims like Mark Spitz."

Steve strummed the guitar. "How do you know that?"

I gasped. And not because of the way Steve looked at me from under his bangs, all cute. "Don't you even know about him?"

"Sure." Steve played a slow version of the Beatles' "Lucy in the Sky with Diamonds."

I tucked my legs up under me. "Haven't you read up on him? Or seen what the news says about him? He was breaking world records when he was eighteen. Mark Spitz might win more than one gold. He's *our* Olympic hero." My mouth kept going and it felt, for a moment, like a runaway train. "I know Nanny's said I wanna swim in the Olympics. But it's more than that. I wanna win."

"She was born with flippers instead of feet," Nanny said.

How embarrassing. "Not really," I said.

"I've seen your feet," Steve said.

And more.

I looked out the window. "Feels like ages since I been in the water."

Steve set the guitar aside. "You were in the Gulf last night."

Nanny drove, determined to make as many miles across Texas, which was a state as big as the world, before nightfall. Even though Steve had done a good job driving the night before.

"I know that," I said.

In the bathroom, mine and Nanny's wet Alamo clothes tried to drip dry. I had on a pair of cutoff sweatpants and a New Smyrna High band tee that Vickie Finlay, cheer captain, threw at me during a pep rally when the high school couldn't sell them all.

"You almost got the body of a swimmer." Steve whispered when he spoke. He leaned against the couch, close enough our arms touched. My skin felt made of live coals and I tried not to move too much. "Legs that won't quit. Not a bit of fat on you. Muscles. But . . ." Steve's eyes were closed. "But you got a big rack."

"What?" I sat up, embarrassed and . . . and something else? Humiliated.

"It's not a bad thing. They look good." Steve sat up now too, eyes open, this slow smile on his face.

"My bosoms are none of your business." I hissed the words at him.

"I'm just saying. Most girl swimmers—"

"I know about most girl swimmers," I said. "Breasts or not, I am faster than any girl on the team. *And* I have slapped down a few guys' records too."

Steve was quiet a moment.

"Gloria Steinem would be sickened by your comment." I stood as Nanny hit a bump, almost throwing me out the side door. If it had been open, I mean.

"I didn't know you are on the swim team, Churchill," Steve said. He stood too, even though the motor home rocked all over, and took hold of my hand. His touch sent an electric current through me. Probably curled my hair more, it was that powerful.

"I'm not. Anyone can time themselves and see where they rate," I said, and shook free of him. I paused then said, "I'm thinking of trying out. I know it isn't the football team and doesn't get all the high school press. But . . ." I couldn't think of anything else to say so I flounced right into the back where I pulled the curtain closed with a flourish. Then I fell on the bed and cried silent tears into a pillow that smelled like Steve.

95

Being Real

Okay, here it is.

The truth.

I swim for myself.

Me, alone.

I never thought of swimming for the Olympics till I saw a picture of Mark Spitz.

But I am fast. And strong. And, as Nanny said, I have flippers for feet. I'm a natural.

An odd thought pushed its way into my brain. Could I be such a good swimmer because of my momma?

96
Apologies

It wasn't but a few minutes later, I heard the curtain slide open. I was having me a conversation with my imaginary Mark Spitz about how a poor, bosomy Southern girl could swim, if she wanted to, if she worked hard, and if she worked out her shy fears about swimming in front of people. Gloria Steinem looked on, arms folded. I covered my head with the damp pillow.

"Miss Jimmie said I could come back here and talk to you if I leave the curtain open and you and me don't get under the covers."

Nanny said that? I didn't answer.

"Look it, Churchill, I was giving you a compliment."

I didn't say anything. I would never talk to Stephen Lovett Simmons the rest of my life. Or at least not the rest of this trip. Or until the next time we stopped for fuel.

"She's looking for a McDonald's so we can get a Big Mac. My treat."

I felt him collapse next to me. I squeezed my eyes tight, and a tear dripped down the bridge of my nose and into the comforter.

"I'm watching you," Nanny called.

Steve didn't move a moment, then I felt him crawl up closer to me.

"I'm sorry, Churchill. I didn't know you were so sensitive about your—"

"Stephen Lovett Simmons, keep your hands where I can see them."

"I'm apologizing, Miss Jimmie, like I said," Steve said to Nanny, and put his hand on the flat of my back, where it felt like maybe a spark might have ignited. He lifted the pillow, smoothed at my hair that I bet looked like a scene from a horror show. He kissed me then, right near my eye. "I'm sorry, Churchill," he said. "I won't ever tease you about your chest again." Then he scooted off the bed and made his way to the front of the motor home as Nanny pulled over on the side of the road, either to kill him, or because she had spotted a McDonald's.

97

Eating Out

The restaurant was too cold, seeing how a storm had swept through cooling off all the land. McDonald's still ran the air-conditioning. I flip-flipped my way across the tile of the restaurant, silent, while Nanny stood outside and smoked and kept an eye on Denny, who dug around in the bit of grass, and Thelma, who stared in the glass door after Steve before surrendering and sulking her way to my grandmother and the rooster.

I hadn't said word one to Steve since his apology, but my insides felt sort of sloppy and happy. He needed to pay. Not for the food. For, well, you know.

We made it up to the counter, where a boy in a light brown uniform and paper cap stood waiting to take our order. His name tag read Mark.

Mark Spitz.

"That a chicken?" he said.

I closed my eyes so Mark wouldn't see me roll them. "It's a rooster," I said.

"And a Lassie dog?"

"What? That's a black Lab." I felt a little disgusted.

"Can I take your order then?"

Steve put his hand on my forearm. "Let me," he said. "Three Big Macs, three large orders of fries, and three big Cokes. The biggest you have. Light ice."

"Anything for the dog or chicken?"

"Ummm." Steve looked at me. I shook my head. "No," he said. "Give us a couple of apple pies. Throw those in there." Steve took a wallet from his hip pocket and pulled out a wad of money.

"Geez," I said, pretending I had forgotten I would never talk to him again, "why do you have so much cash?"

"I always have this kind of dough."

"Geez."

Mark the McDonald's boy raised his shoulders at me.

"We gotta minute before this is done," Steve said. He grabbed my wrist and hurried me toward the back of the restaurant, where a mom and dad with three little boys who all looked the same age crumpled up their garbage and got ready to leave.

Steve pulled me toward the alcove of the bathrooms.

"What are you doing?" I said, "I don't have to—"

Steve's mouth was on mine in a moment, a kiss that sucked the breath from me. I felt his tongue on my teeth.

He pulled me close, turning me so my back was against the wall, and pressed against me. I could feel his heart beating.

"What are you doing?" I said, when he set me free. His face was in my neck. "I been waiting to kiss you since I moved that pillow. I could kiss you all day, Churchill. Where you been my whole life?"

98
Just This Side of El Paso

I wanted to say, *Lugging dishes around your daddy's restaurant with my bosoms,* but I still wasn't talking to Steve. Plus that sounded like my bosoms were doing the lugging, not me. Anyway, at that moment he pulled back, stared into my eyes, like in a movie, and words evaporated out of my brain. Then he grabbed me by the wrist and hurried me to the counter.

"Your grandmother has been watching me like a hawk. It's frustrating."

"Order's ready," said Mark.

Outside, Nanny's cigarette glowed in the late evening. She'd parked the motor home across one whole bank of parking spots.

"Where are we?" I asked Mark. I could feel my pulse in my neck. My lips felt hot. Steve had the tray and carried it to an orange booth.

"A few miles outside El Paso. We close at eleven. That's . . ." He gestured at a clock on the wall behind him then turned and said over his shoulder, "That's a little more than twelve minutes."

"Got it," I said, and went to get straws and napkins from a condiment area. A couple of ketchup packages for good measure and why had Steve been waiting to kiss me and why did I want to kiss him, too, and would Nanny let that happen, not over her dead body, I knew that for a fact, and man! what a kiss and the way he felt all close to me like that. I could hardly swallow.

Nanny was at the door then, Denny in the motor home. Thelma waited on the sidewalk, looking through the glass all sad and sorrowful.

"We're close to New Mexico," she said. Not Thelma. Nanny. She spoke like maybe she had heard me ask Mark. She slid in the booth next to me, scooting me over with her hips.

Steve stood at the small table, tray in hand, then sat down with a sigh. He was picking up the Fletcher habit.

Nanny ate with gusto. "I been telling your daddy a good burger on the menu is a great lunch item," she said. She pointed a french fry right at Steve. "I know the Simmons reputation for loving up a girl and then breaking her heart. You won't be doing that to my granddaughter, will you?"

Steve swallowed a huge bite of Big Mac. I'm not even sure he had time to chew. There was a bit of special sauce on his lip. "No ma'am, Miss Jimmie," he said, and we all set back to eating, me wanting to fade into the plastic of our booth.

99
Real Dreams

So I guess I shoulda known Nanny having her heart broken wasn't going to do me any good. Neither was the fact she had a girl when she was a couple years older than me, who had a baby before *she* wed. Not only did Nanny watch Steve like a hawk, she kept her eyes on me in the form of words of admonition. "No one should give up her dream."

I stared at the tabletop.

She took a huge bite of burger. "Don't you think a ground-beef special like this on the menu would be a great addition?" She licked something from her fingertips. "We could make it a little different than this one here. Not so dry. Thicker. Our own special sauce that's not ketchup and mayo. Homemade potato chips. A side order of fresh-made coleslaw."

Steve finished his burger and then slurped up the last of his Coke. How had he gone through the food so fast? "I gotta get another one, before they close," he said. "I'm not used to grocery-store food." He hurried back up to the counter.

Nanny turned on me.

"I think a burger sounds good," I said, with my own

sandwich caught at the back of my throat so the words came out smelling like food and sounding like I might be hid under a bed.

"I wasn't going to say that," Nanny said. "And you know it. I need me a coffee. I was going to say, don't you dare think I don't see what's going on."

"What?" I bet even the ice in my Coke trembled.

"He has a hankering for you." Nanny dabbed at her mouth. Wouldn't be long before she was applying her lipstick without the help of a mirror. She knows exactly where her lips are, and maybe this is why she was worried about me. Maybe she thinks knowing where your lips are runs in a family. "I have lost my own love. More than once if you include Judith Lee. Plus your real granddaddy." She didn't speak for a second, and I wondered if she said Leon's name in her mind. "I won't see this pain happen to you."

McDonald's felt awful cold. I eyed Thelma, who looked pathetic out there in the parking lot, then back at my grandmother.

"Nanny," I said, keeping my voice low. "You are embarrassing me. Just so you know, I am *not* planning on getting pregnant. *And* if I remember the story right, *you* cheated on Leon and lost him. *Plus* you told granddaddy you were done and he went on his merry way."

Nanny turned till she faced me in the seat. "You think I am worried about him breaking your heart?"

I didn't even have time to shrug.

"I am thinking of *you* breaking your heart. I know how we Fletcher women are. We are women who love with a short fire of flame, if we aren't careful. We do it too young. Fall for the one person we think might make our lives better. That's not always the case. So I am going to be careful *for* you."

Steve was on his way back to the table, this time carrying a bag.

"I'm not in love with him or anything like that," I whispered at Nanny, fast. "I want to be an Olympic swimmer. You know that."

"Got a couple for the road," Steve said, holding the carryout aloft.

Mark passed slow, mopping the floor with dirty water. Nanny tsked, and I could tell by the sound of it she was displeased with the cleaning routine.

"I'm almost done," I said.

"Miss Jimmie," Steve said. He clutched at the bag that seemed to have more than two Big Macs in it. "Look, Miss Jimmie."

"The answer is no," Nanny said. She was up and out of McDonald's, leaving perfect tennis-shoe footprints on the damp terra-cotta floor.

100
Bugging Nanny

I kept eating. Outside I heard the motor home start. Nanny beeped at us.

"You go ahead," I said. "I still have me some dinner to consume."

"She is one stubborn woman," Steve said. "Dad's told me the restaurant's made it through some hard times because of your grandmother."

"Really? I don't doubt that." In slow motion I licked the salt from my fingers. The french fries were cool now. Not as delicious. And the burger sat heavy in my stomach, not unlike a brick.

"You know, I have only eaten at McDonald's a few times in my life," I said, and closed up the remainder of my food to throw it away.

"I'll finish that," Steve said, and pulled the Styrofoam box toward him.

"I've never had that before"—I pointed to my leftover Big Mac—"but I have to admit it was tasty."

Steve finished my dinner sitting at the edge of my seat. His mouth was full of food. How? How could he do that and still look so good?

Mark sloshed past again, and in the rear of the building the lights were turned down.

"We gotta go," Steve said. He wadded up the garbage and stood.

"Not done," I said.

Nanny beeped again.

My heart thumped but I pretended it didn't. Who did Nanny think she was bossing me around like this when I might be on the verge of my first real love.

"Come on, Churchill." Steve offered me his hand. There was special sauce on his pinkie. The crazy thought came to lick the sauce off, but that was disgusting. "Miss Jimmie is gonna get riled. Dad's told me all about her temper."

So they *had* spoken about my grandmother. I felt a bit of happiness flicker in my chest. I took Steve's hand and let him pull me up. My flip-flops felt glued to the floor. Yes, that water was awful looking.

"You like me?" I said, coming up close to Steve's chest. "More than for kissing here and there?"

Who ran my mouth? Who? Was this me being deviant? Was I talking like this because I had given Steve a three-minute silent treatment?

I swallowed. No, I wanted to know.

Steve's arm went around me and pulled me up close.

"I like you," he said, his eyes closed and his voice not more than a whisper. "I like you, Churchill."

101
Keeping an Eye Out, Always

Steve climbed into the driver's seat, and Nanny stood to go off to bed but not before saying, "I am a light sleeper. You pull this vehicle over, I will wake up. You kiss each other, I will hear your lips smack and I will wake up. You do more than drive, and I will wake up."

"Nanny," I said, "you're embarrassing me."

"Again?" she said.

"Still."

Stars flickered on one by one in the night sky.

Steve grinned. "I'm a pretty silent kisser, Miss Jimmie," he said. "I feel like you've offered me a challenge."

Nanny, lips tight as a line, raised her hand at Steve, pointing with her unlit cigarette.

"Don't you push me none, Steve Lovett Simmons. I used to be young once. I know what love is."

"You're still young, Miss Jimmie."

Nanny sort of halted her movements. Then she regained her composure. I saw it happen, as her face sort of melted and then firmed right back up. Oooeee, that Steve Simmons is a smooth talker.

"I know the matters of the heart." Nanny's voice had

lost some steam. "Thelma, come on up with me."

Thelma eyed Steve, sort of looked at me, then walked to Nanny's side, tail tucked between her legs. Thelma's tail. Not Nanny's.

"I'm a straight-A student, Miss Jimmie. My mom and dad don't know that because we don't have the best of relationships and I have kept it to myself. It's one of the things I like about your little family. So's you know, I have only had three *real* girlfriends."

Real? What did that mean?

Nanny wrinkled her forehead. "You're how old?"

Steve ignored the question. "Plus I have never gotten anyone pregnant, like my buddy Jeff Hill did."

"That's good to know," I said. My forehead broke out in a sweat.

"You shouldn't be doing things to maybe get people pregnant," Nanny said.

I raised my eyebrow. Something she should know. Talking from experience.

Steve swung around in the seat. "What I am trying to say is, I'm an okay person, Miss Jimmie."

The sigh Nanny let out should have blown my hair back. "I know that, Stephen," she said, and climbed into the compartment above us. I could see she was bone tired by the way she tried to get up into the bed. "Drive us into New Mexico."

Steve started the engine and shifted the motor home into gear. He pulled away from McDonald's then reached for my hand. "Come sit closer to me, baby," he said.

"And I am listening to you *both*," Nanny said from above us. "I have ears like a hawk."

Steve grinned at me. "I know you do, Miss Jimmie."

102
Waiting

"You're getting all As?" I said. "For real?"

Steve nodded, glanced in the rearview, and reached for my hand again. "Sure am. Hoping for a scholarship to Ohio State. Great football team. Far from home."

I nodded. Almost as good a goal as participating in the Olympics. Though he would be heading into Yankee territory.

"Why haven't you told your momma and daddy this?" I swung my legs around till I faced Steve. I took his hand in both of mine.

He shrugged.

"You do too know."

"I see you," Nanny said. Her voice was tired. When I looked behind us, expecting Nanny's head to be hanging down watching me and Steve, there was nothing. Not that I don't believe my grandmother doesn't have psychic powers or the ability to look through steel with her laser-beam eyes. She knows stuff. She reads minds. That's the truth.

"She's not looking," I said.

"She could be," Steve said, whispering. "Let's see if she is." He tugged me close and I knelt next to the driver's seat.

"Tell me why you don't tell them you are doing good."

"Kiss me first."

My heart pounded in the back of my throat.

Outside the window, Texas was black as an armadillo hole. The moon had fallen over sideways and spilled milky light on the dark road.

Oh, I wanted to kiss him, something bad. But I couldn't always be kissing Steve because he said so. "Tell me," I said.

"Kiss me."

"Tell first." Somehow I had floated a couple inches from Steve's face. He smelled like marshmallows. How was that possible what with all the burgers he'd eaten? Did Colgate make marshmallow-flavored toothpaste?

Steve let out a long breath of air that I thought sure might fog the windshield.

I moved to my seat still holding on to his hand. From above us I heard Nanny in her beginning-sleep snores. We had time.

"Geez, Churchill, I don't talk to people like this." He stared straight ahead, like the black ribbon of road, with its bit of cream moonlight, was the most important thing he'd ever seen. Steve let out another big breath. Glanced at me, all side eyed. "But I guess I can tell you."

103

Truths

I settled in my seat, turned sideways, Steve's hand warm in my own.

"Look," he said, "people don't know this. *No one* knows this."

"Okay," I said.

Steve cleared his throat. "Everyone thinks my mom and dad are perfect."

They do? I wanted to say, but kept my mouth shut. Maybe I was a bit too close to the Simmons family since I bused tables at Leon's and now knew of my nanny's ill fortunes with Leon himself. I nodded instead of speaking.

"So, my mom is like a pillar in the community. She gives all this money to the Elks Club and to charities and she even gave this hunk of change to help with the wing of the children's hospital."

Yup. I knew about Fish Memorial. When I shot a nail through my foot with a nail gun, I visited the children's wing, and I saw a picture of Janet Green Simmons, right there on the wall, cutting a big red ribbon with a giant pair of scissors. Her dog was at her feet like a tiny stuffed animal.

"My mom . . ." Steve's voice went down a notch. "We're

good friends, Churchill. Like, really good friends."

I leaned closer.

"We do all kinds of things together and she surfs with me and takes me places. But. Something's happened."

Steve looked me in the eye. Like stared at me a whole three seconds. I wanted to say *keep your eyes on the road*, but I knew something big was coming, so I kept my mouth shut and stared at him.

"She's leaving. She's leaving us."

It felt like someone had punched me a good one in the stomach. It felt like the time I had been swinging on a tree branch that snapped, throwing me onto my back, knocking every bit of wind from me.

"But—" I said, "but wait . . . Are you going with her? I don't get it."

Steve shook his head. "Dad's dropping her off in Europe. And coming home alone. I wanted to stay here. You know, because of school."

I swallowed. School started in three days.

"I know," Steve said. "If she loves me, why aren't I going with her?"

I couldn't say anything.

He shrugged. "I was supposed to take her to Europe too. I said I wouldn't do it. I thought maybe she would change her mind if I didn't go along. She didn't. She went without me. She went ahead and left." He shrugged again. "That's why I got in the motor home. I'd heard your grandmother talking about leaving when I stopped in the restaurant and then saw her in our driveway. I put it all together, and when she wasn't looking, I snuck on. I needed something normal."

A stolen motor home was normal?

"They fight so much."

Was he going to cry? What should I do if he did?

But Steve didn't cry. He held my hand a little tighter and drove us down that dark Texas road, straight into New Mexico.

104
Too Hard to Hear

We drove in silence for miles. There was nothing I could do or say, but I sorta knew what Steve felt. A little. So I sat quiet and was just there.

105
Getting Closer

The sun edged up behind us.

Way out in front of us the horizon turned gray.

"Mountains," Steve said, pointing with our clasped hands.

"My momma left me too, Steve. I know it's not the same. But I sorta get it."

How could that matter, seeing he had spent his whole life with his momma and she was leaving now. Now that he was almost sixteen. Now that he maybe needed her the most?

That sure wasn't the same thing as what had happened to me.

I didn't know my mother.

I didn't even care about my mother. Mostly.

Steve gave me a smile that was so hurt it took my breath away. "I know," he said.

"I'm sorry," I whispered.

106
Realizing

As I went off to sleep, nodding with the movement of the motor home, I thought, *Now wait a minute. Momma spent my whole life with me till she left. Sure it wasn't as long as sixteen years, but how does any momma leave any baby that's come from her body?* Even in my almost sleep, I couldn't see it.

Mark Spitz was driving the motor home.

"Good thing *you* don't try to drive, Churchill," he said, "'cause you fall to sleep as fast as a newborn."

"Can't help it," I said. My mouth wouldn't move, but I was sure he could read my thoughts.

"You know things aren't what they should be," Mark said. "There's trouble." I noticed the whole driver's seat was wet. There was a pool of water near the gas pedal and the brake. Had he gotten out of the pool? What would Steve's daddy think of that?

"Winston," Nanny said.

"Yes, ma'am?"

"Go get back on the bed. I'm driving now."

I opened my eyes to the bright light of Arizona. "They're huge, Nanny," I said, and my breath tasted like old hamburgers and something worse.

"I'm gonna carry us on into Vegas, baby. And what are you talking about?"

"The mountains."

Steve was sound asleep on the sofa, his hand dragging the floor. Thelma lay as close as she could get to him, her nose under his relaxed fingers. Boy, he was pretty when he was sleeping. Pretty eating a burger. Pretty all the time.

"I know it," Nanny said. "I'm feeling claustrophobic. How could Judith Lee live here?" There was a smile in her voice.

I could see, tired as I was, that Nanny felt happy about closing in on her daughter. "I called her from a pay phone."

I perked up some. "Really? What'd she say?"

Nanny shook her head. The Arizona sun blinded me. It sure was bare out here. Where were the trees? The grass?

"Nothing. She never answered."

I stayed sitting next to Nanny. Swallowed. My throat was dry as ashes. "You thinks she's moved on?"

"Since her last letter? I don't think so," Nanny said. "She has a couple of jobs."

"What time did you call?"

"'Bout five a.m. Soon as I got up to change places with Steve. You slept right through it. Some hoodlum had torn all the pages from the phone book at the 7-Eleven."

Denny sat on Nanny's lap and pecked ground-up corn from her hand. Sure was relaxed driving now. Nanny, not

Denny. I guess that all you need to do is drive across the United States of America and you get yourself some real confidence. Part of me wanted to tell her everything about Janet Green Simmons and her now-used-to-be husband Leon. But I kept my mouth shut.

"Go on back to the bed," Nanny said. "I gotta smoke."

"No smoking," I said. "Feed the chicken." I grinned at Nanny and went off to lie down.

Arizona sun pushed around the shades like sunshine in a mirror.

"I'll never go to sleep. Never."

107
Wrong

I didn't even dream.

108
Close

I awoke to Nanny pulling into some place.

"Gotta clean out the sewage," Steve said.

What kind of world was this? Steve's hand was on my lower back and his breath burned on my forehead. "Miss Jimmie said for me to come wake you. She's taken the animals out. 'No hanky-panky, Steve,' that's what she said. You awake, Churchill?"

Was I?

Steve stretched himself out beside me. Draped his arm across my shoulders.

"Stephen?" Nanny's voice from somewhere outside the motor home. Standing under the back window? Yup, I was awake.

"We're here." His voice was a hot whisper. "Stopped right outside Vegas."

I opened my eyes.

"Hey."

"Hey." I spoke out the side of my mouth so my breath wouldn't get in Steve's face.

"You snore."

"What?" I turned over and sat up. Bright light edged

around the curtains and spilled down the hallway. Were we on the sun? "I do not snore. I'm too young." I slid to the edge of the bed, where I caught a glimpse of myself in a full-length mirror. My hair was a mess—though much more tame than normal—and a red crease ran down my cheek. I wiped at spit, drying my lips on the back of my hand. How embarrassing!

Steve sat up too, grinning. He seemed healed up and haired over since our chat last night. Almost like it hadn't happened.

"You should give a girl a chance to clean up." What was I saying? Steve had been with me all this time, night and day, and had seen me every which way.

"Don't worry. Only you, Churchill, can make snoring and spit sexy."

"You're gross," I said, and hopped up into the little bathroom so I could do my business and brush my teeth. I refused to let myself smile at his compliment. Gloria Steinem would have been proud.

Steve's voice crawled under the bathroom door. "You are sexy, Churchill. Your grandmother doesn't know it, but I coulda copped a feel or stolen your virginity, you slept so hard."

What?

"Get away from the door."

"Don't worry, I got the Lysol spray right here."

"I said, go away!"

Steve laughed. Then he said, "I never thought I would spend part of my summer with such a crazy, foxy family." He tapped on the bathroom door. "You hear me?"

My face flamed the color of a hibiscus. Why did there have to be a mirror right by the toilet seat? "I hear you. Now leave."

"I'm going," he said, and I heard him walk down the hall then open the door to the motor home. It closed with a click.

Sitting on the pot, I stared at my face.

Did I look like a virgin, too? Was that bad? And shouldn't I be a virgin knowing my family's reputation with losing important things?

I shook my head at myself.

Sheesh.

109

Getting Up the Courage

"I think we should sit outside the city limits a bit," Nanny said. She'd already showered, done her hair, had me wash both Denny and Thelma, made Steve change his clothes twice and me three times.

"What's the big deal?" I said. My nerves were thin as wire.

We were trying to find shade, but it seems Vegas doesn't have any.

"She's your momma, Winston."

Steve raised his eyebrows at me as if to say, *Sure is*, or *Look at me and what I'm going through, losing my momma when you are finding yours,* or *Kiss me.* Truth is, I couldn't quite read what he meant.

"Wish we were home watching the Olympics," I said. But I said it real low.

"You gotta respect her for that," Nanny said.

"For the Olympics?"

"For giving you life."

I looked at my fingernails and nodded. "I know, Nanny, but you *kept* me alive."

For a moment I let myself think of me and Momma

(what did she even look like now? All I knew were the last glamour shots from December, mine and Nanny's Christmas present. A lot could happen to you in six or seven months) maybe watching Mark Spitz swim across the screen on our old black-and-white TV back in the Florida room.

Nope. Couldn't see it.

"She's your *momma*, Winston," Nanny said again, and her whisper was fierce.

110

What Makes You a Momma Is Being One

No matter what anyone says, you can't be a momma if you're not a momma.

I'm just saying.

111

This One's for Nanny

At the Shell outside of town, Nanny filled up the motor home.

"It cost us a pretty penny to get here," she said.

I didn't say anything except, "I'm using a real john." The same thing I said every time we pulled into a service station.

"I'll come with you, Churchill," Steve said.

I didn't answer.

Thelma, who is private with her own pottying, ran to the side of the parking lot, looking for grass. There was nothing. "You're gonna have to use the rock," I said.

She gave me an embarrassed look.

"Sorry. I know how you feel. I don't even want to be here."

I slipped across the parking lot, the pavement burning through my flip-flops. And all across my back. And in my heart. A black burn there. Black as hell.

This is for Nanny, I thought. *For Nanny. For Nanny.*

I sure was choosing a poor time to feel unhappy about our trip. Perhaps I should have thought this earlier and stayed home with the chickens. Not that I would have been allowed to do that.

"Your hair looks different, Churchill." Steve had jogged up next to me.

His words melted me. A little.

"Really?"

"Not so . . . big."

"Ummm." How should I answer that?

I stood outside the bathroom door.

"She had an affair."

"What?"

Steve looked toward the pavement. "Lots of affairs."

Thelma wandered around sniffing things. Nanny called her with a low whistle, and Thelma trotted back to the motor home, dodging cars as she went.

"My father said everyone he has ever loved has not loved him enough. Not enough to be faithful." Steve swallowed.

Everyone.

Including my own grandmother. I cooled like I stood in Leon's Deepfreeze.

"Who do I choose?"

I had no answers. Just guilt for something I hadn't done.

Steve grabbed my hand. Pulled me up so close not even a travel pamphlet could fit between us. Right where everyone could see. Right where Nanny could see. The cooled-off part of me melted. I closed my eyes.

"You gotta be nicer to Miss Jimmie," he said. He wrapped his arms around me, put his face next to mine. His skin was hot in the sun. If I touched him with my tongue, would he taste of salt? "This is her girl. Her daughter."

Wait. A. Minute.

The motor home horn sounded. Nanny had seen us.

"Steve . . . you don't . . ." I couldn't end my sentence. I didn't know what he knew about my feelings. Not with this new revelation.

But wasn't he doing something similar with his momma? And his daddy?

Sort of. Kind of.

No, not a thing like this.

I pushed against his chest, but he held on. Not tight. Perfect. I could have pushed him all the way away, but I didn't want to.

"She left me."

"I know."

"And Nanny."

"I know."

The horn blared again. Someone hollered out, "Cool it, sister."

"Your grandmother wants this really bad. So do I." He pressed his lips to mine—a perfect kiss. In front of the whole world.

"Stephen!" said Nanny. "Stop that right now!"

But he didn't. Not right away. He kissed me a little longer, a melted-caramel kiss. Then he walked me to my bathroom door and we went our separate ways.

112
Truth

In the almost-clean bathroom stall I decided that, for the next few minutes, until we met my momma, I would be super nice about what might happen.

Steve was right. My hair looked real good in this dry heat.

113

Tragedy

MURDER AT THE OLYMPICS.

That's what the headlines read on the newspapers. All of them. Front-page news.

That's what people said at the filling station.

My steps slowed like I walked through wet cement. The cement poured down my throat and into my lungs. It hurt to breathe. What had happened? What did this mean? Who would kill athletes?

Who could kill anyone?

The sun was too bright. I was blind.

And all I could think was, *What about Mark Spitz?*

114
Death

Nanny said, "Don't worry," patting at me, but I could see she was scared too.

Black September. Jews. Palestinans.

People kidnapped. Dead.

Mark Spitz is a Jew. That's what my brain thought, but my mouth couldn't say anything. *A Jew in Germany.*

We watched the news on a small TV with aluminum foil wrapped on the rabbit-ears antenna. Everything on the screen looked fuzzy.

All of us, Thelma and Denny included, plus six men and one woman holding a baby, watched. Waited.

ABC didn't know anything about our athletes at the moment.

We'd have to tune back in.

There was a blurry shot of a man in a dark ski mask.

My heart wanted out of my chest. I couldn't feel my hands until Steve locked his own over mine.

They kept saying the same thing over and over.

Black September. Jews. Palestinians.

People kidnapped. Dead.

Dead.

Maybe even Mark Spitz.

115
True Worry

I lay on the bed.
    Looked at the ceiling.
    Swallowed down the worry.
    Cried and waited.

116
Meeting

"We're pulling into the liquor store parking lot, Churchill," Steve said.

I refused to look at him.

"Your mom's gonna want to see you."

"Winston." Nanny's voice cut into the room. The motor home shut down. "I see her. I see her right there." Then, "You stay, Thelma. Denny. Out of the way." I heard the side door open and close.

"I think you have to get up," Steve said from the curtained doorway.

"I know." The sun was too bright for what happened in Munich.

"Think about it later. I'll stick with you."

"I'm not so sure . . ."

Thelma jumped on the bed and nosed right up to my face. "Hey, girl," I said, and the tears fell faster. "You back?"

She hrumphed down next to my body, and I put my arms around her and forced myself to stop crying, my face buried in my traitor dog's neck, her collar jabbing right into my cheek.

117

Doing It

I would do this.

I could do this.

Now. Right now.

"Come on," Steve said, and he slipped his hand into mine, and pulled me to my feet. With his thumbs he dried my face. "I'm not wiping your nose for you," he said. He smiled that brilliant smile. "You can do this."

Yes.

I could do this.

118
Momma

I recognized her right away. It was like looking in a mirror. A grown-up mirror.

"Momma," I said, as Nanny said again, "Judy," and Steve said, "Hot damn, Churchill, now I know what you are gonna look like in a few years and I am even more in love."

"In love?" I said.

Steve grinned in my face. Squeezed my fingers.

Momma was on us before Steve could say anything more. Hugging me and Nanny up so tight I couldn't even pull in a full breath.

"Baby girl," Nanny said, and she was crying. Crying! *My* grandmother. A pecan-size lump clogged up my throat seeing my nanny so emotional. "I been missing you something awful," Nanny said. I could see that was true. Grief and relief were written all over her face. And that missing, right there, clear as words on a Las Vegas billboard.

Denny worked at the hot parking lot, and Thelma kept herself situated in the shade of the camper. Her ears were laid back, and when she caught my eyes over Momma's shoulder, Thelma showed me her teeth. Nope. She didn't look happy, either. Maybe our renewed friendship was already over.

"Look at you, Winston," Momma said, holding me by the shoulders like long-lost mommas hold on to their kids in the movies. Her nails dug into my flesh. "You are beautiful."

I didn't say anything. Just squinted at her. Looked at my momma through a squeezy set of eyes that offered only a bit of sight.

Denny pecked.

Nanny didn't even bother to wipe at her tears. She let them run down her face like she wasn't crying but rejoicing instead. Maybe she was. Whatever, her tears fell like a rainstorm before the tornado weather and I knew if it were possible, Nanny would cry hail.

119
Feeling Reluctant

Momma tried linking arms with me but I wouldn't let her. Instead I latched on to Steve. I expected Nanny to notice and signal with a cough that I should let loose, but she was overcome with her own daughter, who wrapped both arms around Nanny, *my* grandmother—the woman who had cared for *me* since age four—and Nanny didn't even give me a sideways glance.

Sheesh! This was betrayal like Thelma with Steve.

Once sitting in the motorhome, AC running full blast, Momma grabbed ahold of Steve, who turned the color of a ripe persimmon. When I glared at him, Steve excused himself to the potty and came back, his face redder than when Momma held on to him.

What was wrong with me?

Was I . . . could I be . . . jealous of my long-lost mother?

Didn't I want her home?

Ding dang it, I knew the answer to that one. No.

But didn't I want Nanny to be with her girl?

I swallowed.

Yes. Yes, I did.

And no. No, I did not.

Nanny was *my* own, my grandmother-mother. My real momma had left her. Us. She had left me, too. And I wasn't but a little thing.

Now, Momma laughed and chatted like it hadn't been more than a decade since I had seen her.

A decade!

Ten years!

"Let me take you all to lunch here on the Strip," Momma said. "My treat. I'll show you one of the places I work. Two more shows, a few dinner services, and we can leave this godforsaken hellhole."

Nanny eyed Momma. "You mean it, Judith Lee?" Nanny's voice was like a low wind, almost not there, one doing nothing to touch the heat that rose around the motor home, making the distant buildings look shimmery.

"Mommy, call me Skye," Momma said. She smiled like she was posing for an Olan Mills portrait.

Nanny seemed surprised and opened her mouth, then she shut it and didn't say a word.

"You too, Winston," Momma said. "You call me Skye too."

"I won't," I said, knowing I was saying the very thing Nanny wanted to say. Beside me, Steve linked pinkies but I shook him off. It was way too hot for that. *I* was way too hot for finger linking.

This was all Momma's doing.

I reached over and full-on took Steve's hand in my own,

even though we were both sweating. He gave me a gentle squeeze.

"I changed my name, Winston, Mommy," Momma said. She gave the Strip a little nod, like the area approved. Maybe it did. "Some time ago. It's official." Momma swept her arms out. "I am Skye Harper. Let's get this monstrosity rolling on closer to the Tropicana. That's where I work. There's a few places down the street where you can park."

Nanny rubbed at the motor home tabletop, then stood and climbed into the front seat. "Can't believe you did that, Judy," she said. Her voice sounded the size of a dime. "I named you after my dead sister."

Momma let out a sigh and, like that, I remembered.

120
Memories

I remembered the feeling. The always there, uncomfortable feeling between my momma and the woman who had raised me.

I remembered standing between them—little arms raised—saying, "Santa Claus's birds is watching you two."

I remembered Momma saying, "Damn it, Winston, you are three years old. There ain't no Santa Claus, and the sooner you get that into your head, the better."

I remembered loving my momma. And hating her too.

I remembered it all in that little Fletcher sigh of hers.

121

Praying . . . and Such

It was a short drive. Long enough for us to hear the news, and for Momma to say, "Turn that thing off. Let's think pleasant thoughts," so I didn't get me the update I was dying to hear.

She chatted about this building and that one, about some guys named Siegfried and Roy, then spun around to face me, her hair flying like a golden wave.

"Guess what, Winston?"

I shrugged like I didn't care. 'Cause I didn't. Try as I might.

"Guess who I see all the time?" She folded her hands beneath her chin like she was praying. Well, if she was getting all religious, I hoped she'd pray for the sun to dim or the heat to lighten up.

"Who?" Steve said. His hand felt like he tried to send me a message. I shook him loose.

Momma smiled so pretty my heart pinched. Great. I was gonna die of a heart attack out west where I didn't know a soul. Where my dog hated me, my nanny would probably leave me off, and my almost boyfriend decided my momma was beautiful.

Boyfriend?

Had I really thought that?

"You are not going to believe it." She pointed at me and Nanny and Thelma and Steve and Denny, all at once, even though we were spread all over the motor home. "Elvis. Presley."

"No way," Steve said. He grinned in my face. "The geezer can croon."

"Yes, he can," Momma said, then she gestured the way Nanny should go until we came to rest in a parking lot where palm trees waved in concrete planter boxes.

122
So Here's What Happened

We walked all over Las Vegas. It had to be one million degrees, and I felt myself cooking up crispy as bacon, my skin growing tight over my bones.

"Dry heat," Momma said, reaching for my hand the umpteenth time. "More tolerable than in the South."

Ha!

"You think?" Nanny said. "Because I feel like I am going to have a stroke it's so hot."

Momma laughed. Her high heels clicked on the sidewalk. Cars passed, going fast, kicking up dirt and pamphlets that littered the ground. "Maybe we'll get lucky and you'll see him too. The King works right here."

A car full of men passed and hollered something out the window at Momma. She didn't even slow her step. Didn't even look in their direction.

Her fingers touched mine. Her nails were long and polished and her cheeks glowed, like the sun had settled there beneath her bones.

Steve gave my other hand a nudge, letting his own fingers trace where a bracelet might go.

Momma took a tight hold on me . . . and

and
to make my momma
my nanny
and Steve
happy,
I let her.

123
More Memories

There had been good times, too.

Nanny told me them, reminding me as I grew, and I believed my grandmother's recollections and my own soft tugging at the remembrances of sitting on Momma's lap while she read *Where the Wild Things Are*.

Maurice Sendak, Flannery O'Connor, and William Faulkner. My favorites because they had been Momma's favorites. That's what Nanny said. Yup, that good reading had sent me right into the books I'd packed up and brought with me on this trip.

"Winston," Momma said now. She beamed in my face. "You look to be about my size. You wanna try on my feathers?"

Traffic was thick. I felt starved. Feathers reminded me of chicken, which reminded me I hadn't eaten. Which reminded me why I hadn't eaten.

Was Mark Spitz okay?

"What do you mean, your feathers?" I said, when Momma didn't stop staring at me. I made a quick look at Denny but he seemed unconcerned.

She grabbed both my hands in hers and walked backward,

tiptoeing in her stilettos. She looked so young. I had to squint to see her clear. How did she keep the Las Vegas sun from cooking her? "My costume. Let's us all go right now to my dressing room. Marty won't mind."

"I got to get the animals water," Nanny said.

"Mommy, I got water over there," Momma said. She let out a laugh. She sure was happy.

Thelma butted up against my leg, leaving black hair in the sweat there. She looked thirsty with her tongue hanging out like that. If she hadn't been so huge, I would have carried her tucked under my arm the way Nanny held Denny—her little rooster handbag.

Steve still stared at Momma, and now she let loose of me and chucked him under the chin, tying her arm through his.

"What are you thinking, Mr. Simmons?" Momma said. "Don't you look a lot like your old man? What I remember of him. Only better looking."

Steve ducked his head some then said, "You're the knockout."

Momma got all happy around her eyes. She said, "You shouldn't say anything like that to your girlfriend's mother."

"You mean his girlfriend's *Skye*," I said, "and he's not my boyfriend."

No matter what I hoped.

Steve stared at Momma.

I'm pretty sure neither one of them heard me.

124
Show Business

There was more color in this dressing room than in every rainbow the world had ever seen.

"Don't look at the feathers, Denny," I said. I would have covered his eyes, but he was way over there in Nanny's arms. My grandmother walked slowlike in the narrow room that seemed too full.

"Lots of mirrors," she said. "Why do you have so many, Judith Lee?"

Momma grinned from ear to ear. "Skye, Mommy." She waved her hand around, all flappity. "Because this is where *all* the dancers dress. Even us part-timers. When the car broke down, Marty gave me a job. I've stayed near to six months. I got my own mirror that I share with Amber Dawn, my roommate, and everything. I'll show it to you. But look it here."

Momma flipped on a switch, and a row of lightbulbs bathed the area where we stood. The color in the room escalated. Sherwin-Williams couldn't compete in here.

Behind us were costumes of all sorts. Multiples of the same thing. Feathery. Shiny. Sparkly.

Oh, and skimpy.

"You wear those things?" I felt heat rise to my cheeks. Would I ever get away from embarrassing moments? Me, the girl who sometimes went swimming half nekkid? Okay, 99 percent nekkid.

"The girls and me, we get ready for every show right here. When someone can't come in, I take her place. Cool, huh? Winston?" Momma clutched my arm. "Here's where I sit. Try it out."

"No thank you," I said, but Momma manhandled me into her chair. She flipped another switch, and the mirror I sat in front of exploded with light.

"Wow," Steve said. Somewhere in the room I heard Thelma yawn. I agreed with her. "Check this out."

I glanced at Steve. He held a string with glitter and feathers up by two fingers like he had held my bra less than a week ago.

"You're my coloring," Momma said as Nanny said, "That's too big for you, Steve."

125
What I Missed

Momma wanted to paint my face but I would have none of it. "At least try on my shoes," she said after showing me mascara, blush, and then dresses.

"Momma," I said, "I have flippers for hands and feet." Why was I saying this? Why? "I don't want to be a dancer. I want to swim—" My stomach sunk a little. "And your shoes . . ."

Steve stared into the rafters of the room. I noticed there was glitter on his face. Maybe later I would point that out.

Nanny stroked Denny, who slept in her lap. She watched her daughter everywhere she went, like her eyes couldn't get enough of Momma.

"Let's get out of here." I whispered my plea so that Momma had to bend over my shoulder. Her bosoms seemed to grow in the mirror. "Even the dog is bored."

Momma's face—well, she looked hurt.

"What?" I said. I didn't feel even a bit guilty. Then.

Then I thought of all the
lost birthdays
lost nightmares
lost swim practices.

I thought of Nanny walking me in to my first day of school, calling Wiley Anderson's mother after he blacked my eye (for laughing at his name), her late hours at work then helping me with school projects, and hospital runs and staying up late with me.

No. Momma might look all mushy in the face, but she had chosen her path.

One that didn't include me.

Or my grandmother.

"Let's go," I said.

126

She Deserves It, Right?

One good thing about Momma, she was chipper.

My rejection didn't deflate her happiness at all, though I hoped it would. Maybe all the rejection she had gotten in Los Angeles had given her a tough hide, though she looked supple enough. Momma pinched my face into fish lips and tapped her mouth to mine in an awkward kiss.

"Let's get lunch then," she said. "My treat. I know the perfect buffet. All you can eat." She said this last bit to Steve. Like I couldn't eat a lot.

Steve paused then said, "I'm glad about that?" like it was a question and glanced at me.

I nodded in the mirror.

"Yes you are," Momma said.

So was I. I wanted out of this room. There were too many of me everywhere I looked. Bosomy, lanky, eyes too big. And that pouty mouth? Anyone could see I was not happy. At all.

Plus I wanted to see the news. I needed to know what had happened to Mark Spitz and all those other men.

Was he okay? Were the others?

I swallowed at the fear and looked back at the room of

feathers. How could I have forgotten about him and the Olympics? Did magicians share this dressing room too? Had they stolen my memory? Made me forget what was most important?

"Come on, Thelma," I said. "We're leaving." She trotted over to Steve. I stomped across the floor, looking for the door. It took me three tries to find it. How did the show girls—substitutes too—get out of here?

"We'll leave the animals in my apartment," Momma said, then she brushed past me like she was on a mission, and we all had to jog to catch up with her.

127

A Little Bitchy

Steve ran up next to me.

Took my hand.

"Ease up on her some, Churchill," he said.

His words stopped me in my tracks. My feet refused to work and I had nothing to do with it. I felt my face change too. If I coulda shot lasers like Superman, like Nanny, I would have. Two perfect shots right into Steve's forehead.

"What. Do. You. Mean?" I shook free of him. "What do you mean? What are you saying? What do you mean? Are you meaning what I think you mean? Are you?"

Steve stared at me.

"Ummm."

"Um? That's no answer." My eyes had gone so squinty a laser beam might stay contained in my head and burn my own brains out.

Steve raised his hands, like shields. "She's so . . ."

Momma and Nanny walked on. They had linked arms. Nanny looked back once and made a face at me. Momma kept up her fast-paced, high-heeled, I-left-my-daughter-when-she-was-four walk.

"So what? She's so *what*?"

Steve shrugged, tucked his hands deep in his pockets, and turned from me. For a guy who usually sauntered, he sure had picked up the pace when he followed Momma and Nanny.

"Say it!" I said. "Tell me why I should ease up."

Steve turned. He looked nervous—the first time I had ever seen this expression on his face. "You're someone I don't recognize right now. I know I don't know you that well, but you're being a little bitchy."

128
Bitchy?

I stood there on the sidewalk in this strange hot city of Las Vegas. Traffic had picked up, and we were on that main strip of road and the air smelled of exhaust and if we had been any other place in the world maybe the twilight would have shown up, but the evening sky looked like the day sky and I needed to cry, just cry.

Steve wasn't the same as me. Not at all. He had no idea, yet, what it was like for your mother to leave you for your whole life.

The truth was, I hadn't even known I felt like this. So . . . so . . . so . . . pained.

I let myself feel sorrow, deep sorrow—painful, ouch-that-hurts-a-lot sorrow—then I hurried to catch up to my family.

My real family.

My nanny.

Bitchy? Hrmph.

129
Not Having Any of It

I zoomed past Steve.

"No you don't," he said. He grabbed my arm, jerking me to a halt and pulling my arm out of the socket. Well, almost.

"Hey," I said. "Let go."

"I don't think so. You are always trying to get away when you don't like something I do. That's not how relationships work." Steve put his face in mine. "Now, listen to me."

"Why should I?" Why should he talk to me this way?

Heat came up from the sidewalk. Hot as it was outside, I was hotter than fire in the anger area of things. And nice as Steve looked, pretty as he smelled, I would stay mad. Even if his little speech made sense. Which it wouldn't.

"I said, why should I listen?"

"Because." Steve hesitated.

"You're saying this 'cause she has big breasts and is pretty and wears feathers. We got chickens that are nicer than my momma's been."

Steve cocked his head to the side, not unlike Thelma. "I know it," he said. "I know she's hurt you. It's—"

"Winston?" Nanny called. "Steve?" They had stopped off down the road. "You two coming?"

"One sec," Steve called back, and someone driving down the street hollered out, "One sex?" Three girls on the opposite sidewalk, all wearing dresses as short as nighties, screamed, "Say yes!"

Palms trees waved in the evening breeze.

Steve touched my face, his fingers cool, like he painted my cheek with water. "Listen to me, Churchill, for one minute." He swallowed air. "I feel sorry for her. She gave you up. She missed out on something amazing. You. Time she'll never get back. She's trying to get you to like her." He stopped talking then said, "I want that so much from my own mother, I don't want to see you make a mistake."

Did his fingers etch prints into my bones?

Why did he have to make such sense?

I looked off over his shoulder.

"I'll do better," I said, then stood on tiptoe to kiss him.

And what did he mean, relationships?

130
"They Are All Gone"

TVs all over the smoke-filled lobby played the news.

Everyone watched, standing around in half circles. Too much smoke in the room. No one speaking.

What was caught in my throat? A life preserver? I couldn't breathe.

If he was dead . . .

If he was dead . . .

I couldn't think of it. Wouldn't let it be true in my mind.

"They now say there were eleven hostages," Jim McKay said.

What? No. My arms were water.

"Mark?" I whispered the name.

"Two were killed in their rooms."

Murmurs grew. "Hush," someone said.

"Nine were killed at the airport."

"Mark Spitz," I said.

"They are all gone," the news anchor said.

131
But

But.

He was safe.

Snuck away so no one else would die.

132

Heavy

I walked into the bathroom at the buffet, locked myself in a stall, and cried.

Cried until I saw Momma's feet under the door. Her toenails were frosty pink.

"Winston," she said. "Mommy told me about your swimming. Told me about your hero. Come on out, honey, and let me hug you."

I sat there, staring at her feet, a wad of toilet paper in both my hands.

"I got to tell you something, Winston. Open up."

At long last, I did. A crack, a sliver. Momma's eye was there in a second, looking at me looking back at her.

"You know what?" she whispered. "There's a pool right down the road from my place. Let's go skinny-dipping tonight. What do you think?"

I pushed the door open all the way and stepped out. "I prefer to swim in my bathing suit, if it's available."

"Got it," Momma said, then she wrapped her arms around me in an awkward hug, where I cried till I was all cried out.

133
Family

Vegas cooled off when the sun sunk so low there wasn't even a hint of heat left. How could that be? More than a hundred degrees, and now the weather felt like sitting in the motor home, running the AC on high.

My legs wobbled under me.

The night sky was dark as a hole. The light around us too bright. I walked slow, back and forth in front of a doorman.

"I can't believe it," I said.

Steve watched me, leaning against a pillar.

"He's okay. But the rest . . ."

Steve's arms were folded.

"Their families . . ."

I walked quick to Steve. He never budged, even though I stepped on his shoes. "I know what you're thinking. That I need to think of this as a lesson. That we don't know how long we have with the people we *should* love. That I get my mother back and you might not and I am lucky." A breeze cool as water swept past.

He rested his hands on my hip bones. "What I was thinking, is how sexy you are."

"Shut up," I said. But grinned, though sorrow sat heavy over my ribs.

134
Just the Two of Us

Momma and Nanny walked with Thelma and Denny. Steve and I followed. The city stayed alive, though it seemed more drunk people were on the road, wandering, hollering.

"I got to get to bed, Judith Lee," Nanny said. "Skye. I mean, Skye."

Momma smiled all soft-like. "Thank you for trying, Mommy. Me and Winston, we have us a late-night rendez-vous. Do you care if she spends the night with me? If that's okay, we'll take the four of you on back to that house on wheels and she can grab her things. How does that sound?"

Nanny glanced at me and I gave her a bit of a nod. I wasn't expecting a sleepover, but . . . when I glanced at Steve and he looked so hard into my eyes, I felt my insides go mushy.

"Sounds good. I need to rest up." Nanny's voice came out low and so un-Nanny-like. So . . . what? . . . content? Not that she hadn't been content in New Smyrna, but there was always an edge to her there. Maybe being separated from a daughter you knew was worse than not having a momma you didn't know.

"Steve, you can come with me and Winston next time we go swimming."

"Yes, ma'am."

"This time"—Momma swung Nanny's hand—"is for us two." She looked at me over her shoulder.

We were to the motor home now. Nanny unlocked everything, and I went in to get my swimsuit. I slipped it on in a bathroom that seemed too small after the wide open feeling that being free from the motor home a few hours gave me.

I looked at myself in the mirror.

Terrible things had happened today.

There was good news, too. Sure.

But that awful stuff. Those awful moments. Those families changed, forever.

And now, now I was going to go swimming with my momma.

My family.

My heart picked up a beat, and I hurried on out to where Momma waited.

135

Rogue

"We squeeze through here. Me and Ryan—I met him a coupla weeks ago, he works on stage crew—we've come here a few times."

I pushed through the gate.

"Now we have to be quiet," Momma said. "They close the place down at one."

This was exciting. Wait. What was going on with me? I stopped, hesitated. Stealing, kidnapping, and now trespassing. Okay, I was a seasoned trespasser. Still, was I turning into a hardened criminal who enjoyed her illegal life, running from one hazardous adventure to another?

I shrugged. This wasn't as bad as the other crimes. Trespassing in Vegas was something to be added to my rap sheet. "Can we get in trouble?"

Momma shook her head. "No one's ever gonna know."

136

More Night Swimming

The water was soft as silk, and one thing became clear to me. I did not get my fishlike swimming abilities from my momma. All Momma did was sit in the shallow end on the steps or dog-paddle.

Still, I loved it. I loved being with her and hearing her whisper, that soft voice floating on top of the pool water, telling me what a great swimmer I was and how she was sure, sure, Mark Spitz woulda been proud of me.

That she was too.

Proud. Of me.

137
The Jitters

When we walked home, leaving wet footprints on the still-warm Vegas sidewalks, Momma bumped me with her shoulder. "You a bed hog?" she said.

"Maybe. It's hard to say. The only one I ever share a bed with is Thelma. She's the one hogging all the room. I sleep on the edge when she's sharing with me." Too many words came out because I was nervous.

Nervous.

Who ever thought of someone being nervous with their own mother?

The moon was bigger and brighter than any I had ever seen. And white, white, white.

"I guess we'll have to see," Momma said. "We're about to my place. Shoot, swimming sure does make a girl need to get her beauty sleep, doesn't it?"

I looked at Momma to see if she was serious. She seemed to be.

"It does," I said. "Though after a long day in the ocean I sometimes feel like my bed is a series of waves, rocking me to sleep."

Momma let out a big ol' sigh. "I miss New Smyrna Beach.

Miss the sand and the crash of the waves, real waves, and that oceany smell that water has."

I crossed my fingers, something I hadn't done in years. "When we get back home, maybe you and me can go swimming there." I said the words so slow maybe Momma didn't even remember what the last word I spoke was. I was surprised sounds even came out of my mouth. I hadn't known I would say it.

Momma looked at me. "I'd like that," she said.

And the strangest thing was, I knew I'd like it too.

138

Settling In

I rinsed off while Momma pulled out the sofa bed and made it up.

"Me and Amber Dawn take turns getting the real bed. Two weeks at a time," Momma said when I came in from the bathroom. She was propped up, reading, one of the sofa cushions supporting her.

"What's that?" I pointed to the thick book.

"East of Eden," she said. "You might like this one. It's all about family heartbreak." Momma set it on the coffee table, then flipped off the light.

I stood stone still. Did she know? Did she know Nanny's heartbreak?

"Remember when I used to read to you?" Momma said, her voice right-away sleepy.

I nodded though she couldn't see me, and climbed into bed, slipping as close to the edge as I could. "I do remember."

"Winston," she said when we had both settled down. "Look it. I know I did a bad thing leaving you. I want you to know I ain't planning on being your momma when I get back home with you and Nanny. I want to be your friend. That's all. You okay with that?"

I swallowed at sudden tears. "I am," I said.

139
Dream

There was a gunshot loud as glass exploding.

"I seen you with that boy *and* with your mother." Mark Spitz had a thick southern accent, like he was born and bred in Louisiana. He carried a shotgun and aimed at ducks that seemed to come from nowhere.

"I like your hat," I said. "It looks good on you." That was a lie. Mark wore a huge pink sun hat. One a woman would wear to New Smyrna Beach.

"You best keep swimming alone," he said. "They are all gone."

"What?"

But he had slipped away.

140

Talk

Momma and me had breakfast at Denny's. Denny's the restaurant, not Denny's the rooster. Then we hoofed it back to the motor home, where Nanny and Steve played cards.

"Getting ready to go on the floor and play a few hands," Steve said. He looked so pretty I wanted to reach over and sniff his neck. "Come sit by me, Churchill," he said, and patted the seat next to him.

"Thelma's there," I said.

Thelma looked up at me and showed me her teeth.

I bent near her. "I love you," I said, stroking her head, "even if you have betrayed me." I expected Thelma to show Steve which card to play next, but she leaned against his arm and sighed.

Nanny gave me a look, and I went over to kiss her cheek. "It was fun," I said.

Nanny seemed like she might bust wide open she was so happy. "That's terrific, Winston."

"Mommy," Momma said. She wore crisp white shorts, and her legs were tan and long when she sat on the sofa. "I saw our girl swim last night and she is fine."

"She is," Steve said, and he and Nanny folded up their cards and packed them away.

I grinned. Two great compliments.

"Olympic material," Momma said.

Nanny tsked. "What is the world coming to?" she said. "The whole of Germany is in an uproar. But the Americans are all safe."

"Thank goodness," I said, and I meant it with all my heart.

"She should have swimming lessons," Momma said. "With someone who can really help her improve."

Nanny nodded. "Costs money."

"I know it," Momma said. Then she went quiet.

"Hey," I said, "swimming in the ocean's the best training for me there is."

Momma eyed me.

"If I get past the breakers, I work against the tide."

There was an awkward silence, and then Nanny said, "Let's go sightsee then get you packed up, Ju—Skye."

"Okay, Mommy."

So we got.

141
Packing

Let me say this, you can look at only so many building fronts before you start getting bored.

And let me say this, too.

Momma has a lot of stuff.

A. Lot.

142

A Break

"I got to get me some air," Steve said, when Momma started on her tenth box to be packed up.

Nanny was saying, "Really, honey? That too? Where you going to wear *that* in Florida? At Leon's?"

Momma looked at Nanny with these wide eyes that seemed to say, *I haven't given it much thought.*

There was still so much work to be done.

"I got to get some real air," Steve said again. "Let's go swimming, Churchill."

"Huh?" I stared at Steve. He seemed a little wilted.

Nanny, on the other hand, was in her element, lifting, folding, organizing.

Momma sat back on her heels, head tilted, like she saw the world in a whole new way.

"Swimming?" I said, "In the middle of the day? Where?"

Steve stood. "*Any*where," he said.

I glanced over to Momma and Nanny. This feeling, this huge *I want to be a family, a whole family* came over me. For a second I couldn't move. Then Steve laced his fingers through mine.

"Momma," I said, as I walked to the door of her little

apartment. My voice was a whisper. All those families missing someone they would never get back.

She looked at me. How could she pack wearing high-heel shoes? Tears blocked my throat. "I'm glad you're coming home with us," I said. "I've missed you something awful."

143

What I Didn't Know
I Had Even Been Missing

That hug? That was the best hug I have ever gotten from my momma. Including when I was little.

144

In My Element

Outside, the sun wanted to fry my retinas.

Steve pulled me close and we bumped sides. "We can go to any ol' pool," he said. "As long as there are people there, no one will know if we're staying at that hotel or not."

So we did.

And I swam, back and forth, back and forth, back and forth, thinking about my new family, and possibility sat like an anchor in my chest.

145
Jewelry

Momma worked that night, and me and Nanny and Steve and Denny and Thelma all tried to get her boxes stored in the motor home.

"We could pull a U-Haul trailer," I said, "like she did."

Nanny looked like someone had dipped her in boiling water. "I don't think so. Add an extra fifteen feet to this motor home and who knows what ditch we'll end up in."

"There will be lots of people to drive," I said.

"Your momma won't be able to make it to the highway without complaining," Nanny said.

"What?" I blinked. "Are you sure? She drove from Florida to California and then from California to here."

Nanny stared at me.

"All I'm saying is she has some traveling miles under her belt."

"All I am saying—" Nanny's unlit cigarette dangled from her lips. It had been a few days since I had seen her fake smoking. "—is that your momma cannot be trusted on the road, and this thing is worth a billion dollars more than you and I have."

The evening cooled down fast. Over in this part of town

where Momma's apartment stood, the city wasn't so bright. I could see the stars, the closest I had ever seen. I handed a box off to Steve, who pushed it under the motor home into a huge storage compartment.

"I could almost pick you one," Steve said. "Set it on a gold chain." He stretched long and his shirt rose on his stomach. He reached for my hand, our fingertips touching.

"What are you talking about?" My face colored and I wasn't sure why.

"A star," he said. "I could almost get you one."

"Why would you do that?"

Steve relaxed against the motor home, crossed his legs at the ankles. "A star would look good on you, Churchill."

I was to him in three steps, pressing against him, knocking him off balance a little. Steve's arms went around me, loose, like this was the way we were meant to be. Star or no star.

146
How?

How could horrible things, awful things, *and* great things happen all at once?

How was it fair that the world kept turning? Going?

I pressed my face into Steve's neck, grateful.

147

The Last of It

It took forty minutes to load the motor home, what with the hugging in between box moving.

"I bet we are going to be over the weight allowance for road safety," Nanny said when Steve locked the side compartment.

Momma gave a laugh then scooped me up. "I need a hug before Steve takes them all for himself," she said. "I am so excited to get on the road. So excited to see home."

Nanny, who looked like to bust out of her skin from happiness said, "I can't wait till we're a family again either. I have been hoping for this day. Waiting a long time."

I rested my head on Momma's shoulder. She sure did smell good.

"Hey," I said into Momma's ear. "I gotta tell you something."

She held me at arm's length. "What's that, Winston?"

"Later."

She kissed me on the forehead. "Later then," she said.

148

Said It and Glad I Did

I stood outside Momma's apartment. Steve waited on the sidewalk with Thelma. Nanny and Denny were taking their own midnight stroll.

"It's been a long day," Momma said. She smiled at me, and her teeth looked like pearls in the moonlight.

I nodded, my heart thrumming. "Look it," I said. "You have to be careful with Nanny."

"What do you mean?" Momma said.

I pulled in air enough to maybe start a hurricane. Or maybe it would calm the hurricane I felt growing in my stomach. Why was I scared to do this? To talk to Momma like someone should have talked to her years ago?

"Say it, Winston," Momma said.

"Okay then."

Behind me I heard a car horn sound and there was a screech of brakes. Amber Dawn shouted for Momma to shut the front door. The two of us moved onto the porch.

"Go ahead."

"Nanny's been waiting for you to need her a long time, Momma. If you break her heart, you know, by not coming home with us, who knows what will happen to her."

Momma seemed stunned. Her mouth opened and closed. "Winston, whatever made you think I'm not coming along?"

I shrugged. What *did* make me think this? Anything I could point to? Anything I could touch? All the horror of the past few days. All the good?

"Winston, girl, I am coming home. With you."

"Really?" Relief spread out to the very end of my hair. "You promise?"

Momma nodded. "We leave after I finish my shift and get my paycheck tomorrow. We are on our way."

149

No!

And here came Steve, running, out of breath though he and Nanny and Thelma and Denny hadn't been that far away.

"She's been hit," he said. The words were hollow. Frightened.

"Nanny?"

"Thelma."

I couldn't move at first. Then we were both running, Momma left behind, cold air, cold blood rushing through my body.

Is she dead? I wanted to ask but I wouldn't. Couldn't.

On the road ahead, I saw a few cars stopped, headlights cutting into the darkness, and Nanny kneeling in one lane, another person near her, Denny hopping back and forth. People standing on the sidewalk, watching.

"No, no! Thelma!"

I could smell the road, the cars' exhaust. Thelma didn't move.

Nanny glanced over her shoulder. "Stay back, you two," she said. She sounded tough, her normal Nanny self. "Don't look."

But I didn't listen.

I pushed past Nanny. The pavement felt too warm under my hands and knees. Thelma's eyes were open, her tongue out. I crawled next to her. "Thelma?"

Nothing.

"Nanny?" My voice was the beginning of a scream.

My grandmother touched my shoulder.

"I didn't mean to hit her, kid," a man said. "I didn't see her. I'm sorry."

I put my face close to Thelma's, that scream rushing up from my toes. Panic taking over every part of me. "Thelma. Thelma." Her pink crocheted collar looked dirty. She needed a bath. I should have given her a bath.

I should have made her presentable.

My dog. My best friend.

150
Almost

Then Thelma let out an almost-not-there whine.

151
The Hospital

I cried all the way to the veterinarian emergency care, holding Thelma on my lap, who didn't look at Steve at all. She stared at me. Every once in a while she made a feeble attempt to lick my tears.

The man who'd hit Thelma drove us to his pet's clinic, crying the whole way too. Turns out he was a dog man.

152
Tomorrow

The vet said all she needed was a cast and a stay overnight.

"We'll pick you up tomorrow, Thelma," I said, burying my face into her fur. She rolled her eyes at me when I kissed her forehead.

153

A Dare

"Kiss me, Steve."

"Not in front of the dog."

Thelma played Steve's guitar.

"Come on."

"Your grandmother will know."

"Since when did you care about that?"

"Since we met."

I awoke with a start.

Thelma!

My heart slammed against my ribs.

The motor home was dark, and cool Nevada air blew through the open windows.

Nanny slept in the bed over the front seats.

From the back came "The Sound of Silence." Guitar.

Nanny would never know . . .

I tiptoed to the back, the song growing louder as I moved closer. My lips tingled. I stood, quiet, outside the curtain.

"Come on in, Churchill," Steve said.

I started. "How did you know I was out here?" I whispered the words.

"I was hoping you'd visit."

I pulled the curtain open. Steve sat propped up on the bed. His shirt was off. He set the guitar aside. "Come here," he said, and I crawled up to where he was.

154
Caught

I hadn't kissed him even five minutes when the curtain was nearly torn off the track.

"Y'all," Nanny said, and she breathed the word like the world was made of fire. And then: "Go."

So I went.

155

How People Get Babies

When I was on the sofa bed, and Nanny back up in the rack, I said, "How'd you know?"

"I heard your lips smacking," Nanny said. "And it better never happen again. Kissing in a bed ends up with you having babies and then those babies end up taking off to California to become a star."

"Oh," I said. I was quiet a moment. I sat up, folded my arms around my knees. Denny settled himself in his box. "You ever thought, Nanny, that I might *not* take after you and Momma?"

Nanny was so silent I was sure she had gone to sleep. I listened for her snore, but instead she slipped down to where I sat and plopped on the bed next to me.

"I guess I don't give myself much credit for raising you, do I? I figured I failed with myself and then I failed with my daughter. That means I would fail with you, but I guess that's not always the case, huh?"

Outside, a semi roared past and the motor home swayed.

"I guess not." I felt a little indignant. "You know I don't want to do what you or Momma did, Nanny. I have plans. I want to be a swimmer. Go to college. And besides"—I played with the sheet—"I've seen what heartache does to people. I've seen on this trip how you wish there were lots of parts of your life that was different."

She nodded in the dark. "That's true."

"And anyway, me and Steve haven't kissed each other that much."

Nanny stood, slapping her hands on her knees. "And I want to keep it that way. Stevie, you get on back in bed. I see you hiding out down there at the end of that hall."

"Okay, Miss Jimmie," Steve said.

They both left.

156
What We Are

We were scheduled to leave at three thirty, after Momma's last lunch service at the Tropicana.

Me and Steve and Nanny and Denny did everything we needed to get ready.

We made a grocery run.

We filled up with gas.

We dumped off the sewage (gross!).

We picked up Thelma.

We washed the sheets and our clothes at the Laundromat.

Nanny counted out her money, which, she said, would get us back home if there were no more troubles, but I could see the worry between her eyebrows. Last night's doctor visit hadn't been figured on.

Steve and I kissed in the shady side of the motor home. He smelled like vanilla and I couldn't figure out why. But I liked it. Liked his lips on mine. Liked his hands touching me. Liked the way he ran his fingers through my hair even though they'd get caught in the tangles.

"Churchill," Steve said later, resting on the steps below the side door, "I am so glad I came on this trip with your family."

"You are?" I petted Thelma, who was still letting me give her love. Scary as it was, that broken leg made her want to be with me more.

He nodded. "Sure am."

"Why's that?"

The sun was hot enough to fry my eyelids. Thelma's hair stuck between my fingers. Her cast was clunky and gave her a limp.

Steve stretched out long, and I slid closer to him so he could wrap his arm around my shoulders. "You're all about loving each other."

"What?" I looked at him, surprised.

"I see this fierce love between the three of you"— Thelma looked Steve in the eye—"I mean *four* of you. I don't think I have ever seen that at my house. Just watched Dad take all Mom had to dish out and thought that was the way it was supposed to be."

Inside, Nanny was singing an Elvis song.

"I like all the love about your family."

I nodded. "Me too." And man, I meant those words. I sure did.

157

Eighteen Minutes

"She's late," Nanny said after a while. "Eighteen minutes late."

By now I was checking out everything we had crammed into the fridge. I needed something good to eat. Grapes would do.

"Not yet," Nanny said. "Don't eat anything till your momma gets here."

Steve shuffled the three decks of cards he'd bought at a casino. "Think my dad would like it if I came back to Vegas to be a blackjack dealer?"

Nanny didn't answer. She stood at the door, looking out in the direction of Momma's apartment.

I popped a few grapes off a stem and went to put them in my mouth.

"I said no, Winston." Nanny's voice had no energy. No oomph.

"Now, Miss Jimmie," Steve said. "Don't you get upset yet. Eighteen minutes isn't that long. Why, my mother is sometimes three hours late for things."

But Nanny didn't answer.

158
Knowing

When she was one hour late, Nanny said, "I think we ought to think about unpacking Judith . . . I mean Skye's . . . stuff." Nanny didn't move when she spoke.

"Are you kidding?" I said. I felt sick to my stomach and not because I hadn't eaten.

"Look," said Steve, and he pointed off down the street. "There she is. Right? Isn't that your mom, Churchill?"

"I think so. Nanny, you see the girl hoofing it toward us?"

Nanny didn't move. Not even to look. She sat still on the sofa.

"What's the matter?" I said, putting my arm around her shoulders. "Nanny, she's late. Here she comes."

Nanny looked me in the eye then. "Winston," she said, "you are the best part of my life that there is. The best thing that ever happened to me was your momma leaving you with me."

I smiled at my grandmother. Swallowed a couple of times. For a second I felt like I couldn't breathe, the way it sometimes happens when a wave surprises you, and holds you under the water like a hand. "You're the best part of mine," I said, when I caught my breath.

159

A Part Revealed

"Sit down, sit down, sit down one and all," Momma said, hollering when she was half a block away.

Her voice was what? Excited?

My stomach rolled over.

"Mommy! Mommy! Mommy!"

By now I could hear Momma's high heels clipping on the sidewalk.

"I got it! I got it!"

Momma filled the doorway. She cast a shadow in on all of us, like something had covered the sun. Thelma growled but didn't try to get to her feet.

"I got the part on *General Hospital*!"

It took me a moment to understand what Momma had said. She'd gotten a job at the hospital? The vet clinic?

"The call came. I have a one-year contract! They want me in California tomorrow! If the world loves me, my character won't be killed off."

All five of us looked at Momma.

"Wait," I said, getting to my feet. "Wait. You're not coming with us?"

"I'm not," Momma said, shaking her head. "But did you hear my news?"

Nanny didn't say anything for one whole minute, then stood and went to her daughter. She caught Momma in a hug and held her close. "Congratulations, Skye," she said. I almost didn't hear her.

"Wait," I said again. I felt like a broken record. "Wait. We drove all the way out here to get you. Our dog almost got killed because of this trip. Denny's losing feathers."

Momma, hand clasped with Nanny's, went to sit. My grandmother's face looked flat.

"They'll have a ticket waiting for me at the airport."

"We talked about this," I said. "You and me, we talked. Just last night."

"I know, Winston," Momma said, "but this is my dream come true."

What about Nanny? What about her dreams? I couldn't swallow.

Momma turned, facing Nanny. "Do you think you could stay one more day and drop me off at the airport?"

160
Results

When it was all over

    when Momma had gotten all her stuff back into her apartment and

    worried over what to pack and

    what to wear and

    the flight and

    if she would be able to memorize her lines

    we left her at her apartment where Amber Dawn just couldn't believe it and

    I watched my nanny walk the slowest I have ever seen her go, right to the motor home, where Thelma and Denny waited.

161
The Ache

Nanny didn't say a word after we dropped Momma off at the airport.

She drove until the sun set and then changed places with Steve

who didn't try to kiss me once

and if he had, I would have only kissed him a little.

162
And More Results

There was no word about the Alamo, about the Gulf of Mexico, about Mark Spitz, about the loss of eleven athletes, about Leon's restaurant, about the chickens at home, about our having stolen a vehicle to pick up a momma who had decided to stay out west, about our dog in a cast, about anything.

I bet me and Steve could have rolled all over the floor kissing and smacking and saying "I love you," and Nanny still woulda kept her mouth shut.

163
One Change

"You stopped smoking," I said to Nanny as the sun set on us in Alabama. We were hours from home.

Nanny glanced at me, her eyes full of tears, and said, "Thanks for noticing, Winston."

164
How Did I Feel?

How did I feel about Momma doing what I, somehow, knew she would do?

How did I feel about Nanny being so heartbroken?

How did I feel about me?

Losing my momma again?

Well, I felt awful for my grandmother. And achy at what I had lost.

165
Real Friends

In Daytona, Nanny and me and Steve cleaned the motor home from tip-top to bottom.

We vacuumed, washed, and sanitized. We threw away garbage, got dog hair and rooster feathers out of corners, and buffed all the windows till they shone.

"Listen, Miss Jimmie," Steve said when we got back up on the road, "my dad and mom don't take this vehicle anywhere. You know I'm covering for you if they even notice."

Nanny smiled with her mouth, but not a bit of happiness leaked upward toward her eyes. She looked like she was in pain. "I'm gonna tell your daddy what I did," she said. Nanny sucked in air. "Then I am quitting Leon's."

"What?"

I wasn't sure who had said the word, me, Steve, or Thelma.

"What do you mean, Nanny?"

My grandmother didn't answer for a good half mile, and I knew better than to ask again. New Smyrna was getting closer and closer.

"I mean," Nanny said, slowing down as we drove the old canal road, "that I am tired of living a lie. I thought your momma would come home with us, Winston, and I was wrong." Nanny swallowed so loud Thelma looked at her. "I have loved your daddy, Stevie, for I don't know how many years. I'm not putting myself through it a minute more. I'm getting me a job in Orlando."

I was speechless.

Steve seemed to be too.

Only Denny had something to say, and I think it was that he wanted to get back to his chickens. He seemed a little wilted. He even had a few bald spots.

Truth be told, we all looked a little worse for wear. Traveling all over the United States of America, even with the foxiest boy in all of Florida with you, and doing it in just a few days, sure was draining. Add a stupid mother into the mix, and a traitor dog with a broken leg and horrible world events and the end of summer and us coming into school a few days late, and the whole thing seemed like a wasted trip.

166
One Thing to Be Thankful For

Thank goodness there had been plenty of kissing.

167
Advice

"Talk to him when he gets home, Miss Jimmie," Steve said. "I got a feeling my dad's trip to Europe didn't work out that good."

168
Results

Mark Spitz won seven gold medals. Shane Gould got three golds, a silver, and a bronze.

I couldn't get the blurry photo image of the man in a black ski mask out of my head.

Thelma's leg healed so she only had a limp.

Denny stayed bald in a few spots.

And Nanny went to talk to Leon, who came home from overseas, where he had watched the Olympics and Mark Spitz swim to victory, without his wife.

169

Moving On

My first real day to high school my sophomore year, I came into the halls long before anyone else and a week late. I'd been to check out the swimming pool (they wouldn't let me in, not even to practice on my own, because swimmers take priority, but I was thinking of maybe *becoming* a swimmer and if I didn't, I still knew that secret way in) and now I stood at my locker, spinning the dial on the lock.

Patty Bailey almost knocked me off my feet when she ran up and hugged me. "Hey, girl," she said, "we got math and physical science together. I am so glad you are home. Man, do I ever have things to tell you."

She smelled all vanilla-y and wore fat bell-bottoms that covered clunky clogs.

I grinned right in her face. "Me too," I said. "I got some things to tell you."

Not a bit of it had to do with Nanny, but I would, for sure, mention Steve *and* my momma. No need to tell her the felony part of things, though.

"Catch you third hour," she said, and clomped off in a crowd of kids she was at least one head taller than.

I opened my locker and slipped my old notebook in.

Nanny had come home late the night before. Too late. I'd heard her crying in her room. Thelma stood outside Nanny's door, whining, but Nanny never opened to either of us, even though I whispered to her that everything would be all right.

"It's okay, Winston," Nanny had said, and her voice could have broken my heart right in half. "I promise it's okay. We're not going to Orlando after all. This is me missing your momma, that's all."

Now, I turned to head to class.

The halls crawled with students, but there was Benjy Aufhammer and a couple other football players—wearing lettermen jackets despite the heat.

Steve came up to me, appearing from behind his friends like an angel (where *was* Angel?) and looking so nice my heart didn't beat. Or maybe it overbeat. Is that even a word? I hadn't seen him in two days, since we'd pulled the motor home in his driveway, and he'd dropped me and Nanny off at our place. And even though the hall was crowded with more kids than should have been allowed in one place, seeing Steve was like a movie. A slow-motion, blurred-at-the-edges love story where only the two of us existed.

"Hey, Stevie," I said. Everything on my body felt awkward, even my ankles. I touched my hair. Since when did *I* care about the way I looked?

"Winston," he said. He dropped his books, grabbed me

so tight I didn't even try to breathe, and kissed me in the biology wing of New Smyrna High.

"Get a room," someone called when the kiss went on as long as a real movie kiss, and someone else let out a wolf whistle.

"I been waiting to do that since I drove away Wednesday," he said, his breath hot on my neck. Then he kissed me again, before I had the chance to say, *Well, I'm glad you did.*

170

Being Related to Someone Famous

Momma, it turned out, was *General Hospital*'s new star. And everybody who knew Nanny at Leon's had something to say about it.

Busing tables, I heard Mr. Wilson say, "That daughter of yours looks like a mirror image of you, Jimmie. Can you believe she's made it big? What do you say you and me go to the Dew Drop Inn for a nightcap."

"I cannot, Randy," Nanny said, and I wasn't sure if she meant no to Momma's stardom or no to the offer of a drink. "You need your ice tea topped off?"

Doris said, "Maybe your trip out to Vegas turned out to be the good-luck piece that girl needed."

"Maybe," Nanny said.

Miss Clealand said, "Jimmie, Judith Lee has become such a looker. I always wondered if she would grow into those buckteeth of hers and she more than did."

"Skye," Nanny said, and Miss Clealand looked at Nanny like she had lost a few marbles.

It seemed everyone talked to Nanny about the one thing she didn't want to hear.

At home, Nanny refused to speak to me about anything

that was important. Including Momma. And her late evening with Steve's daddy. Or how I was doing in school and whether I had made the swim team and how me and Thelma were doing in general.

It was like we had left the most important part of Nanny back in Vegas on the Strip—her heart.

171

Another Letter

Nanny was at work when I pulled the letter out of the mailbox.

Misses Momma and Winston Fletcher, the envelope said, *605 East Lake Drive*.

There in the corner, *Skye Harper, your momma and daughter*.

I'm not kidding. That's how she addressed the envelope.

I stepped out of my school clothes and put on my busing uniform (no bra, shorts, T-shirt, apron). I tucked the letter into the big pocket and started on foot and in a hurry to Leon's restaurant.

172

And What . . .

Steve met me halfway to work.

"Something's getting ready to happen," he said, after he'd pulled to the side of the road to pick me up. Led Zeppelin screamed from the eight-track. Steve turned the music down a little. "Why didn't you call me to give you a ride?"

"Are you kidding?" I touched Momma's correspondence. What was she writing so soon for? We hadn't been gone from Vegas even two weeks. I climbed into the car.

The sky was overcast, heavy with clouds. A September storm was on its way. A hurricane maybe? Or a tornado?

"Huh?" Steve said.

"I mean, of course I wouldn't ask you for a ride. I've always gotten to Leon's on my own or with Nanny."

Steve looked at me, eyebrows raised. "Why not? Aren't we . . . You know."

I stared at him. "Aren't we what?"

"You know." He stopped at a red light, then shrugged. Someone behind us beeped when the light changed and we still sat there. "You know." Steve drove on.

I'd run out of spit. "What are you saying?"

"Some people are meant to be together, Winston. Like you and me. So next time, call me." He took my hand, lacing his fingers through mine. "Now listen."

I smiled at him. Fingered the letter with my free hand.

"My dad called and told me to make sure Miss Jimmie was going to be at the restaurant."

We were almost to Leon's.

I gasped. "Why?"

"I don't know. That's what I told you when you got in the car. Something's going to happen."

"What? Do you think he'll try and buy her out?"

Maybe we were moving to Orlando after all. My nose holes closed up and I became a mouth breather right then and there.

Far out over the ocean, lightning splayed like limbs on a tree. The water and sky were a smudge of gray on the horizon.

"I don't know," Steve said. "But my father has never asked me to do anything like this before, not even with my mother."

173
Will . . .

Nanny was there already. The old Blue Goose was parked under a streetlight.

As we pulled into the lot, Leon Simmons drove in too. He didn't see me and Steve. He ran inside the restaurant.

Me and Steve? We followed his father, fast as we could.

174
Happen?

Leon caught Nanny in the Deepfreeze.

Shut the door when he saw me and Steve standing there, waiting. Nanny's eyes were huge. The last thing I heard her say was, "You know we can get locked in here, Leon."

And him, "I don't give a damn, Jimmie."

The restaurant grew busy, and waiters and waitresses ran around, taking orders and filling water glasses.

"You could help," Doris said to me, but I pretended like I didn't hear her.

"What does he want with her?" I squeezed Steve's hand till he kissed my knuckles, each one, and said, "Relax," but I could see he was just as nervous.

I kept thinking how in all my life I had never really even met Leon Simmons. I had only seen him as I came in for a shift and he left. I had watered the plants at his house. Kissed his son. Gone swimming in his pool (*almost* nekkid). Driven around in his motor home. But had never even said more than a hello to him.

And now Leon Simmons had locked himself in the freezer with my grandmother.

175

?!

"He asked me to marry him," Nanny said when she walked out of the freezer.

The kitchen went dead quiet.

Leon grinned.

"Dad?" Steve said.

"What are you looking at?" Nanny said. I closed my mouth.

Doris, who'd come in to see where the front-end manager was, let out a whoop. "What did you say? What did you say?" She was screaming.

"Perhaps," Nanny said, and then she clapped for the workers' attention. "Let's get going. We have people to feed."

176

Here's the Thing

Some stories have horrifying ends, even when there are seven gold medals.

Some end well. Like this one.

So I wasn't about to ruin Nanny's happiness by pulling out that letter from Momma.

177

Hope

"He said"—Nanny drove one-handed toward home—"he had missed me all these years. That we were meant to be together. That some people are."

Steve's words. To me. "He did not."

"He did."

My face warmed up.

"You think it's true?" I whispered the question. Hoping for both of us.

Nanny nodded. "I do."

"And?"

"And he said he forgave me years ago, but that I had never forgiven myself."

Warm night air blew into the car windows. The storm had passed us by, dropping only a smattering of rain.

The letter was still hidden away in my pocket.

We'd open it tomorrow.

178
Truths

"Dear Winston," Thelma read. "You will be dating your brother if Nanny marries Leon. As you know, that is against the law."

"Don't say that," I said.

"Plus you may have to serve Denny up in a stew at the restaurant."

"Stop it." My voice came out slow and thick as Karo syrup. "That's not true."

Thelma thumped around my room on her back legs, even though the one was still in the cast. She waved the letter around with her front paws. "It's my job to keep you honest."

"May I take your order?" Mark Spitz said. He wore my apron, and the medals hanging from his neck blinded me.

179

The Last Letter

I sat right up.

Thelma looked at me from the floor. Her cast kind of glowed in the moonlight.

I grabbed the letter from under my pillow and ran to Nanny's room.

"Hey," I said, poking her in the shoulder.

"Lions and tigers," Nanny said opening her eyes. She cleared her throat. "What do you need, Winston girl?"

"There's a letter here from Momma. It came today."

Nanny sat up like she was a part of the Siegfried and Roy magic show. "What did it say?"

I sat on the side of her bed. "I haven't read it."

180

But Not the End

Dear Mommy and Winston,

I just wanted to say to you 2

Thank you!!!!!!

And tell you I love you. PLUS can you come out to California at Christmas time??? I'll git YOU this time. No motor home trips. Plane tickets. Steve can come too.

Mommy, you were there for me all my life.

Winston, I want to get to know you. Even if I am living my dream. Because guess what? A dream ain't that great if a little girl ain't there to share it with her mom.

I better go.

Love,

Skye Harper

181

It's Never What You Think

Nanny held my hand.

"I wasn't expecting that," she said. "No, I wasn't expecting that."

182
Well, Almost Never

Neither was I. Not in a million years.

183
Promises

I was almost asleep when there came a tap at my window. "Winston," Steve said.

I got up and tiptoed over. I parted the curtains, smiling.

"Hope it's okay. I had to see you."

I pressed my hand to the screen. "Hey."

"Come outside. I have to show you something."

Quiet as a girl and a dog with a cast on can be, me and Thelma hurried outside.

Steve sat on the front porch. He grabbed my hand, pulled me in the yard. "Look," he said, and pointed at the full moon. An arch of white painted at the sky.

"A moonbow," he said. "I've never seen one before, and I thought I should share it with you. You know, before our lives change. It means promises. Just like a rainbow."

"It's beautiful," I said. I breathed the words out.

Steve bent to kiss me.

"Y'all!" Nanny said. "Stop that!"

But this time, we didn't.